RED CROSSES

Sasha Filipenko

RED CROSSES

*Translated from the Russian
by Brian James Baer and Ellen Vayner*

Europa
editions

Europa Editions
1 Penn Plaza, Suite 6282
New York, N.Y. 10019
www.europaeditions.com
info@europaeditions.com

Translation by Brian James Baer and Ellen Vayner
Original title: КРАСНЫЙ КРЕСТ
Translation copyright © 2021 by Europa Editions

Library of Congress Cataloging in Publication Data is available
ISBN 978-1-60945-693-1

Filipenko, Sasha
Red Crosses

Book design and cover illustration by Emanuele Ragnisco
www.mekkanografici.com

Prepress by Grafica Punto Print – Rome

Printed in the USA

This novel, with its interweaving of past and present and its juxtaposition of the highest moral standards with the basest acts of violence and betrayal on the part of individuals and of the Soviet state, creates the impression of a complex musical composition. Indeed, musical works appear throughout the novel, from Russian pop songs to Listz's *Hungarian Rhaposody*, not to mention the graveside cross that turns into a musical instrument at the first gust of wind. The "orchestration" of the novel is largely carried out through a layered narration, involving Sasha, the main narrator, who speaks in the present tense without quotation marks, his neighbor, Tatyana Alexeyevna, whose narration is in the past tense and introduced with a dash, and a third, omniscient narrator, who often takes over Tatyana's narration of her past or interrupts her narration to comment on it. Dialogues between Sasha and Tatyana are formatted with double quotation marks. In order to make this complex interweaving of voices and temporal frames more visible and to highlight Tatyana Alexeyevna's narration—as she is in many ways the soul of the novel—we decided to format her narration in italics rather than with dashes. Such a graphic representation of the narrative planes is in keeping with the author's use of historical documents, which appear intermittently throughout the novel and include internal Soviet government memos, official Soviet decrees and rulings, as well as telegrams and letters from the archives of the International Committee of the Red Cross, all in their original formatting.

Those documents are indicated by a change of font. There are also several poems, mostly Russian, and popular songs, which we indented as block quotations.

It should also be mentioned that the city of Moscow is a major character in the novel, and while it is typical in tourist literature and historical documents to transliterate Russian place names, such as the Moscow street Kuznetsky Most, those names in Filipenko's novel often assume a symbolic resonance when they are connected to the novel's themes. And so, because bridges is a running motif in the novel, second only to crosses, we decided to translate the street name as Kuznetsky Bridge Street. We followed a similar logic in our treatment of punctuation, specifically the ellipsis. Ellipses are used with much greater frequency in Russian than in English and often for different purposes, for example, to mark a change of topic. Moreover, Filipenko uses ellipses at a rate that is high even for Russian to serve his artistic ends. We, therefore, retained ellipses that were used for reasons very specific to this novel, namely: to indicate pauses, as when Tatyana Alexeyevna is searching for words or trying to recall events; to allude to some especially horrible consequence or impending occurrence the speaker cannot name; or to mark the interruption of one narrative thread, which will be picked up again later.

In concluding, let us say how very honored we are to have had the opportunity to translate a work which offers what is undoubtedly one of the most courageous and unflinching looks at the Soviet past, alongside a deeply humane portrayal of two individuals attempting to reckon with that past for the sake of their future, and ours.

Brian James Baer and Ellen Vayner
January 2021

To Konstantin Boguslavsky, with gratitude
for his help in writing this book.

RED CROSSES

After the signing, this odd woman—odd the way all real estate agents tend to be—says to me: "Congratulations! I'm very happy for you! Why so gloomy? I've gotten you the best quality for your money!"

The agent takes a lipstick from her purse and, no longer paying any attention to her now former client, continues to prattle on:

"We have what they call a win-win situation. By the way, who are you planning to live with here?"

"My daughter," I answer, looking outside at the playground in the courtyard.

"How old is she?"

"Three months."

"How nice! A young family. Trust me, you're going to thank me again."

"For what?"

"What do you mean for what? I've already told you. You're so forgetful. You only have one neighbor on this floor. And she's a lonely ninety-year-old woman with Alzheimer's. You've really hit the jackpot. Make friends and get her to sign over the apartment to you."

"Thanks," I say for some reason, continuing to look out the window.

The apartment's empty. There's not a chair, bed, or table. I begin unpacking my bag. The former owner is having a hard time leaving. She stands next to the window trying to smooth down paint ridges on the windowsill and driving her memories in circles as if ironing a sheet. Why bother—I'm going to change everything anyway.

"Will you be staying here alone tonight?"

"Yes."

"Where are you going to sleep?"

"I have a sleeping bag and an electric tea kettle . . ."

"You can stay at my place if you'd like."

"No thanks."

The woman gives up. I'm too young for her. Leading the former owner by the elbow, the agent finally leaves the apartment. Left alone, I sit on the floor.

This is it, I think, this is an ending. One life has ended, and another life is beginning. Transcendental zero. At almost thirty, I've become a man whose life has been torn in two. I'm being offered a new beginning once again. How could I object to that? Suicide's not for me, especially now that I have a daughter.

I probably won't remember my thoughts from this evening. There's fog in my head, dust dancing on a beam of light, and nothing else. I take a short break before starting my second chance at life. My first life has ended, and the second one is about to begin. It's an abyss with a suspension bridge over it in the shape of a man. If you want to get to the other side, you have to throw yourself across the abyss. My mom likes to say that happiness always has a past, and that sadness always has a future.

Like a shipwrecked sailor thrown onto an unfamiliar shore, I decide to explore this new island—the city of Minsk. Why did I come here in the first place? It might be a neighboring country a lot like my own, but it's still foreign. There's a red Catholic church and a wide avenue, a statue of some balding poet and the Palace of the Republic, which looks like a mausoleum. There are dozens of new buildings and not a single memory—only unfamiliar windows and alien faces. What is this country anyway? What do I know about this city? Nothing, except that my mom lives here with her second husband.

There's a pile of discarded books in front of my building. One catches my eye: *A New Land* by the Belorussian writer Yakub Kolas.

I climb up to the fourth floor, and on my front door I see a red cross, not big, but bright. It must be a joke by the real estate agent, I think. I leave my groceries near the elevator and begin washing the cross off the door when I hear an unfamiliar voice behind me:

"What are you doing?"

"Cleaning my door," I answer without turning around.

"Why?"

"Some idiot drew a cross on it."

"Nice to meet you! The idiot you're referring to is me. I was recently diagnosed with Alzheimer's. So far, it's only affected my short-term memory—sometimes I don't even remember what happened a few minutes ago, but my doctor promises that very soon my speech will be affected too. I'll begin forgetting words and then I'll lose the ability to move. Not much to look forward to, huh? The crosses are here to help me find my way back home. But pretty soon I'll probably forget what they mean too."

"I'm sorry," I say, trying to be polite.

"That's okay! It's the only way things could have ended up in my case."

"Why?"

"Because God's afraid of me. I have too many inconvenient questions for him."

My neighbor leans on her cane and sighs deeply. I keep quiet. God is the last thing I want to talk about right now. I say goodnight to the old woman, pick up my groceries, and am about to enter my apartment when I hear:

"Don't you even want to introduce yourself?"

"Alexander. My name's Alexander."

"And how long have you been talking to women with your back turned?"

"I'm sorry. My name's Sasha, and here's my face. Goodbye!" I answer with a fake smile.

"Does that mean you're not interested in knowing my name?"

It's true, I'm not interested. Gosh, what an annoying old woman! What does she want from me?

I need to get home. I want to close my eyes and finally wake up. This trick has worked for the last thirty years. In the past, scary, terrible things happened to me only in my dreams and never in real life. I was happy and had no worries. Not a care in the world. The last few months have been rough on me. Dammit, I just want to get some rest!

"My name is Tatyana . . . Tatyana . . . Tatyana . . . oh, no . . . I forgot my patronymic . . . Just kidding! My name is Tatyana Alexeyevna. I'm very happy to meet you, you ill-mannered young man!"

"But I'm not."

"Really?"

"Not really—it's just that none of this really matters right now. Excuse me, it's been a hard day."

"I understand! We all have hard days. Hard months, hard lives . . ."

"It was a pleasure to meet you, Tatyana Alexeyevna. I wish you all the best—happiness, good fortune, and all of life's pleasures," I say sarcastically.

"You know, all those things are just starting to happen to me . . ."

God dammit, this is getting really irritating! First it was the real estate agent, now this old woman. I don't want to talk, and I'm sure my neighbor senses it. She realizes I'll take advantage of a moment's pause, so she talks nonstop.

"True, all this will be finished rather soon . . . in a month or two. Very soon there'll be nothing left of me in terms of my life story. The fact is, God's trying to cover his tracks."

"I'm very sorry," I say, despite myself.

"Yes, you've said that already! I forget everything pretty quickly, but not that quickly! May I see how you've set up your new place?"

"To be honest, the only furniture I have at the moment is a toilet and a fridge. There's nothing to show. Maybe in a week or two?"

"Would you like to see how I live?"

"Well, it's already getting late . . ."

"That's okay, Sasha, come in!"

I'm not thrilled, but I obey the old woman's wish. In the end, it's silly to argue with someone who has only half a brain left. The neighbor pushes her door open, and I find myself inside her apartment.

There are canvases everywhere, and it looks more like an artist's studio. The paintings don't look like anything special. I've never liked this kind of art—endless pale colors, desperation in every inch of the canvas, faceless people and colorless cities. But I don't know much about art.

A dark-gray square canvas hangs in the middle of the living room.

"Are you starting a new painting?" I ask for no reason, trying to fill a pause.

"What are you talking about?"

"The canvas on the wall."

"No, it's finished."

"Oh, really! And what does it depict?

"My life."

Ugh! Here it comes—break out the violins. Old people tend to exaggerate their misfortunes. My life . . . Pass the tissues! They think that bad things only happen to them. I almost blurt out that, in respect to hardship, I can teach a lot of people a thing or two, but I stop myself just in time.

"Of course, I've been told that Minsk is a gray city, but I've never thought it was that gray!"

"There's almost no Minsk in this painting."

"I'd say there's not much of anything in that painting."

"So, do you think I'm wrong when I say it's my life?"

"I don't think anything . . ."

"You're thinking: 'I was going home, minding my own business, and there she was—a crazy old lady whining about her fate?!'"

"Is that what you're going to do?"

"Aren't you interested in the least?"

"To be completely honest, no, I'm not."

"Well, you're wrong. I want to tell you an unbelievable story. Not even a story but a biography of fear. I want to tell you how horror can suddenly take hold of a person and then change their entire life."

"I'm intrigued, but maybe next time?"

"You don't believe me? Oh, well . . . You know, a little more than a year ago I was standing where you are now. It was December 31. It was snowing, and the twentieth century was coming to an end. It was literally ending, that's no exaggeration; there were only a few hours left. The Kremlin clocks were getting ready to strike twelve, and, pumped full of drugs, the president of the country next door was getting ready to announce that he was tired. In the kitchen, everything was as usual—the TV was on, and something was burning in the oven. I wasn't expecting anything special; it was just another New Year's. How many of them had I already lived through? Yadviga would call me, but nobody else. I'd eat something nice and watch a New Year's program on TV. I'll celebrate New Year's in Moscow first, then in Minsk. In short, I wasn't expecting diddly squat from the end of the century, but suddenly the doorbell rang. It's probably the neighbors, I thought. A very nice, friendly woman lived in your apartment before you—a true daughter of a communist. Her father was a low-level party bureaucrat, but she was all right; she'd grown up modest and decent. She'd always give me that puppy-dog look, as if apologizing. I thought she'd come by to ask for some salt or something like that, but I was wrong. It was the mailman, can you imagine! A real mailman came to my door on December 31. And he brought me a letter that I'd been waiting half my life for . . ."

As soon as my neighbor says "half my life," I wake up. For the first time this evening, I'm present. Before that moment I've been just hanging around, but now I begin paying attention.

I looked at the envelope lying on the table—it was an ordinary envelope. I'd been waiting for it for half a century but couldn't bring myself to open it. I was more afraid of this piece of paper than I'd ever been afraid of anything in my life. I finally took a deep breath and ripped it open. It was the letter! I burst into tears, then rubbed my eyes and sniffled. I didn't touch that piece of paper again and called Yadviga instead.

"I got the letter! He's alive!"

"You're kidding?!"

"No, I'm not!"
"Is he far away?"
"About two hundred kilometers from Perm."
"I'll go with you!"
"Let's go."

I called the airport. The operator was very nice and wished me a happy new year.
"There's a flight to Moscow at 10 P.M. Can you make it?"
"I can, if I don't die first."

After Yadviga arrived, we had some tea and called a cab. The dispatcher said we were lucky—it was New Year's Eve after all, and all the cabs were usually taken. "Can I have a look?" my friend asked, and I gave her the letter.

We locked the apartment door and went out into the courtyard. A taxi-driver was standing there next to his cab. He opened the trunk but didn't help us with our bags. "I'm a driver," he said, "not a porter."

We arrived at the airport and found the ticket counter. We were panting, out of breath. "Don't worry," the girl says. "You have plenty of time! When you arrive in Moscow, you'll have a layover of several hours."

"When was the last time you flew?" I asked Yadviga.

"Never," my friend answered.

Well, there we were, two old women on New Year's Eve flying into the unknown . . .

The flight to Moscow was fine, but the second flight was bumpy. The airplane was shaking as if God were kicking it. We couldn't land on the first attempt, and so the plane started circling the airport again. The passengers were going crazy; I remember, some were screaming. A man in front of me was *howling like a dog, but I didn't blame him for that—fear is a very complicated thing. And I know what I'm talking about.*

We'd just gotten our bags when a heavyset man approached us:

"Where are you headed?"

"Here," I said, showing him the envelope.

"You know, that's pretty far. I'd say, it's three or four hours away. But you're lucky—my dad lives near there."

"If you could take us to the bus station . . ."

"What bus are you going to find on New Year's Day?"

We arrived in the little town in the morning. It was still dark, and an armless statue of Stalin, covered with snow, was freezing in the square. "Why is his head so small?" I asked.

"Well, the old one got chopped off. They ordered a new one at the regional center, but the sizes got mixed up. There's no money for another head, but, anyway, no one's going to replace it until this one gets chopped off, too. Where are you planning on staying?"

"We don't know," I answered.

"If you're not afraid, you can stay with my old man. He's not a bad guy, you know. He was sent to prison here. After he was released, he didn't know where to go, so he decided to stay here and work as a guard. I was born here too, on the other side of the barbed wire. My mother passed away three years ago. I moved to the city a while back. So, who do you know here?"

"A man," I answered.

My neighbor stops talking. She falls silent for several seconds, long enough for me to think that I'm witnessing one of her blackouts, but then she comes back to life and says:

"I was born in London in 1910 . . ."

+

lexey Alexeyevich Bely was a kind man of deep religious convictions. He met Tatyana Alexeyevna's mother in Paris in 1909, during Diaghilev's Russian seasons. Tatyana's mother, Lyubov Nikolayevna Krasnova, was a ballerina and died in childbirth. Two women were put in charge of raising the baby: a Frenchwoman, who taught her religion, and an Englishwoman, who was responsible for her posture.

His wife's death drastically altered Alexey Bely. Previously good-natured and trusting, he changed in a single day, severing all ties with the church and devoting the rest of his life to fighting ignorance. Or so he thought . . .

According to my neighbor, her father was a neurotic. Literally every little thing drove him to distraction. If, one morning, a stranger wished her papa a good day, he would break into a broad smile and go on for hours about the heights of refinement achieved by British society. But if the opposite occurred, and someone was rude to him, her father would sit in front of the fireplace and philosophize about the imperfections of this world.

Alexey Alexeyevich would often visit the nursery during her lessons. He would settle into an armchair and then interrupt the governesses: "There is definitely no God! Our sweet old lady has lived too long in antediluvian Russia, whose only achievement was to reconsider the minimal number of fingers necessary for venerating spirits. There is no God, my child, and there is no soul! People are just another species, a species not unlike, say, horses or dogs. Some are of the opinion that we're more developed . . . Well, in some sense that's true—we've learned how to build bridges, steamboats, and omnibuses, but this where all of our achievements end. The soul that your sweet nanny is talking about is nothing more than a trap for our brain, not a bad one, but nothing more than that. There is no heavenly kingdom and no life after death because nothing exists outside of our thoughts. The mind is not a weapon, it's our main problem. We make a fatal mistake when we assume that we can understand something. Rephrasing Descartes, I'd say that a man exists only when he's mistaken. Your mother died the day you were born, and she will never reappear anywhere. There is no resurrection or any other such nonsense. There's only heresy and lies. We should think of ourselves as representatives of a species that did not previously exist and that will cease to exist in the future. Every second, in this never-ending continuum, our brain is busy deceiving us. When offering us hope, our brain is surely making fun of us. Strictly speaking, my dear, self-deception is our distinguishing characteristic."

In 1919, Alexey Alexeyevich decided to go to Russia. He entered the room and cheerfully announced, "We're leaving! Old people live here in London. In Russia there lives a new kind of person—which I'm too old to become, but which you, my dear, definitely will."

After voicing this rather strange opinion, Alexey Alexeyevich took a gulp of whisky and left the room. The move had been decided.

For a drinking man, Bely was surprisingly practical. He always carried out his plans and solved all his problems. In moving to Russia, he deliberately avoided using the word "return." Tatyana Alexeyevna's father insisted that they were going to a totally new country that had no precedent in the history of mankind. Well, in this he was to some degree correct.

I think this was the first uprising I had the chance to observe: Our sweet nannies flatly refused to move.

"Such foolish dears!" father said, smiling. "Don't you understand that this is your country now?! How can you not understand that what's taken place in Russia is not just a change of government but a revolution of the spirit? Petrograd and Moscow are now cities of the common man. Everything there is organized to improve the lives of ordinary people like you."

Ordinary people . . . Papa often repeated: ordinary people. An impregnable combination of words, don't you think? An ordinary person . . . What is that? A parasite who does mean things or a nameless hero who performs a feat of bravery? An ordinary person . . . How many of them have I had a chance to meet? Fate has presented me with hundreds of versions but has never given me the correct answer. At one point, I thought an ordinary person was someone bad because at various times in my life I was surrounded only by bad people. Meanness was their behavioral norm. But no sooner had I become convinced of this than completely different people—people who were outstanding and pure—suddenly entered my life. Probably the most precise definition of an ordinary person is anyone, but over time I rejected this definition too, as fate led me to cross paths with several absolutely amazing individuals . . . But anyway, anyway, this is all idle talk! Forgive me, Sasha, I've digressed. So, what was I talking about? Oh yes, I was telling you about my nannies. Perhaps they understood that Moscow had all of a sudden become a city of ordinary people, but they had no intention of going there. On the verge of hopelessness, they presented their last, and as they saw it, their strongest argument:

"Alexey Alexeyevich, it's okay not to think about us or about

yourself, but what about little Tanya? Do you really want to destroy her life? Haven't you heard about the horrible things that are happening in Russia? Wouldn't it be better for you to go there alone, and then, if you find life there to be as you've described it, we'll bring Tanya next year?"

"No!" my father said sternly. "We're leaving as soon as possible!"

+

The move took place at the beginning of 1920. While reasonable people were leaving the country, the Belys were moving in the opposite direction, toward the storm, into the epicenter of history. They didn't meet any new or fundamentally different people, but on the first day they came across three marching bands.

"What are these marching people so happy about?" the nannies asked in surprise. "They have no water, no gas, no electricity. All they have to brag about are government-issued cigarette holders that freeze to their lips!"

"Just wait, my dears!" my father said cheerfully. "Let's see what you have to say in a year."

"You promised that we were coming to a country where ordinary people are happy, but all we've heard about so far is uprisings."

"Fools! I'm telling you, just wait a year!"

There was famine in Moscow. But Tatyana Alexeyevna's father seemed untroubled by that. There were certain people who were constantly helping his family out. Alexey Alexeyevich never called them by their real names; in conversations he always used aliases. Tatyana remembered only two of them: Old Man and Lukich. She didn't understand what exactly her father was doing, but it seemed that his frequent business trips to Europe were a matter of national importance.

At night, after putting the little girl to bed, the nannies would whisper in the next room:

"My God! Doesn't Alexey Alexeyevich see? Why doesn't he understand that it's impossible to change or to save these people? He's constantly talking about new people, but doesn't he see that these new people are sprouting from dead soil? Of course, the Reds won't hold on to power. I'm sure there will be total chaos here for decades to come."

"I don't know . . ." the French nanny would answer. "It doesn't seem so stupid to me anymore. It looks like Alexey Alexeyevich is indeed more astute than we are. The royal family has been executed—this country will never be the same. I think the Reds won't leave. It's hard to believe that Admiral Kolchak visited us in London just a few years ago, and now they've put him down like a dog."

"What's even harder to believe is that Alexey Alexeyevich is on the same side as those people. Oh, we can only hope that it doesn't all end in tragedy . . ."

Unlike her nannies, Tanya liked Moscow from the start. Like Alice in Wonderland, she'd fallen into a fairytale dream.

"The provinces of humanity," her French nanny would say sarcastically.

"The suburbs of common sense."

"A government that has yet to have its confirmation ceremony."

While her nannies were practicing their witticisms, Tanya was studying Moscow with great interest. Dinners, Borjomi mineral water, appetizers, and drinks. Newly hatched Soviet people. Bigmouthed comrades beating drums and waving red banners. The nannies would cover their ears while little Tanya, frozen in place, would try to read the words written in white letters, "Proud of our newly installed machinery!" How about that! Tanya would look at the people, wishing she could carry such a huge red flag. And really, how could a child not like a country that was building infantilism?

Every day they went to the newsstand. While Soviet men stood in line to buy *Pravda*, her nannies bought *Znamya*, *Moskva*, and *Severnoe Siyanie*. After completing their daily ritual, they would take this mountain of paper and go on their walk. It was all so thrilling! And Tanya would periodically come to a halt in order to sound out some new word.

"What is Pro-let-kult?"

"It's not important!" the old women grumbled in unison.

They sent me to 'The Fourth,' an experimental school of aesthetic education. A semi-boarding school. They kept us busy all day long. General education subjects were before lunch; drawing, eurythmics, and sculpture—after. One evening, a friend of Papa's asked me where I studied, to which I replied, "In a school for the children of gifted parents." A rather accurate slip. In reality, it was exactly that. They didn't take just anyone. Only the progeny of the Soviet elite studied there. When the ordinary citizens of this new country heard our parents' surnames, they'd pass out, but what did we care? Kids will be kids . . .

While Tanya sculpted squares, her father, Alexey Alexeyevich Bely, spent all his time in Europe. In 1924 he had to move again, this time to Switzerland. Bely traveled between Geneva and Berlin, and Tanya, despite a gaggle of new tutors, was left to her own devices. Bern, Lausanne, Zurich. Castles, mountains, cities. She traveled through Switzerland with her new tutors and couldn't imagine that one day she'd return to Moscow.

Tanya spent the spring of 1929 alone. Her papa stayed mostly in Zurich while she spent her time in Ticino, in the Italian-speaking region of Switzerland. Bellinzona, Locarno,

Chiasso. With her drawing paper and chalk pencils, she would travel to a new little town almost every day. Once—for some reason she now thinks it was on a Sunday—Tatyana went to Porlezza, a small Italian village on the border with Switzerland. A dozen stone houses, and one and a half churches. Everything was as it should be: wine, sycamore trees, and the tolling of the bells. She was drawing on the quay when a handsome young man approached her. He was tall, with black hair and olive-skin, and he suggested they go for a walk. "Why not?" Tatyana Alexeyevna thought. Their conversation consisted of jokes, the history of the village, and a discussion of the new man. Nothing special—an idle but charming exchange. She told him about Russia, and he confessed that he'd never even been to Milan. They spent the whole day chatting, and Tatyana, realizing she'd missed the steamboat to Lugano, decided to stay in a little albergo on the tiny Via San Michele.

They had breakfast the next morning. Coffee and unbelievable pastries, so good you'd sell your soul to the devil for them. He was looking right at the bridge of her nose, and, embarrassed, she looked down. That same day they got some stale bread from a small restaurant and went to feed the swans that were sitting on the grass. She looked at the lake and tried to record it in her memory, as it seemed to her there would never be anything better. And when the bats came out at night, she wasn't even scared—it was so peaceful there.

A few days flew by. The young lovers hiked in the mountains and fished, dove off the cliffs, and kissed. Tatyana understood that this Italian would be her first man, but unfortunately, on the evening when it should have happened, an awful thing occurred—Tatyana Alexeyevna Bely sneezed.

Some phlegm fell on the sand, right near our feet. To put it crudely, a huge green ball of snot flew out of me. It was so embarrassing! I wanted to run away, but I was so ashamed, I couldn't move. Can you imagine a more horrifying situation? Just think about it: a girl, she's in love, and suddenly there's this ball of snot!

Romeo tried to be a gentleman. He stepped on the phlegm and began rubbing it into the sand, but this only made things worse. Now the snot was not only on the ground, it was on the sole of his shoe. Romeo smiled, tried to make a joke, and asked how to say it in Russian, but Tatyana broke down in tears. Never before had she cried so hard. Romeo tried to hug her, but she pushed him away and ran toward the hotel.

For several days, Tatyana Alexeyevna cried in her room. Romeo stood under her balcony, but Juliet didn't open the blinds. Juliet had a runny nose and a fever of 102; she was mortified. A doctor came to visit her and, seeing the various pills in his pretty leather case, she wanted to swallow them all. After the doctor left, the concierge knocked on her door. A stranger, he was nonetheless concerned, and asked her to have pity on the unfortunate Romeo and let him in. A Russian family had moved into the room next door. White emigrés, they would spend hours discussing the role of great literature. Having run out of money, they couldn't continue those conversations in Switzerland, and so they took their discussion of the purpose of Russian literature to this Italian village. Sitting in her room, Tatyana Alexeyevna leaned against the thin wall, wiping her runny nose while listening to the idea that the task of Russian writers was (first and foremost!) to demonstrate the capacity and range of the great Russian language. Before her eyes was the image of Romeo spreading her snot across the sand, while a woman on the other side of the wall kept insisting that a writer must speak broadly and powerfully while protecting tradition. "We don't have great books anymore!" the woman behind the wall concluded. "Our novels, except for Papa's, are dull and extraordinarily simplistic. We live in an unbelievably barren age. In the last few years we've seen (I repeat, not counting Papa's book) maybe one or two good books, two or three decent ones, and about five that are passable."

While Romeo was spreading her snot across the sand, Russian literature was withering away. Romeo was rubbing a ball of phlegm into the soil of Italy, while great Russian literature was atrophying. While Romeo moved his foot back and forth, like a dancer, Tanya began to realize that she was miserable and in love.

The night before my departure, my beloved climbed through my window. I began screaming so loud, he only had time to toss me a letter before jumping back out the window. From his note I learned that he would wait for me all his life, that he'd wait for me not in Verona, but here, at Lake Lugano, in the small Italian town of Porlezza. "Okay, we'll see," I thought.

"But did you recover?"

"What?"

"I'm asking if you got better. Did your cold go away?"

"Ah, the cold . . . No, not really. I didn't get better, but I left. Papa sent his assistant for me, and on my way to Zurich I learned that my father was ill. 'He's not in critical condition, but the doctors suggest that he go back to Russia, just in case.'"

"In case what?" I asked.

"You'll see for yourself," the driver answered . . .

Her father was dying. A case of pneumonia turned into a family tragedy. Even though no one spoke about it, everyone understood that they were going to Moscow to bury Alexey Alexeyevich. Several weeks before his death, using his connections, he'd managed to enroll his daughter at the university. That's how in the fall of 1929, her second fateful trip to Moscow occurred.

+

At the end of her first year at the university, a nondescript man approached Tatyana Alexeyevna. The man took her aside and asked:

"How many languages can you speak?"

"Who are you?"

"Answer!"

"French, Italian, English, German, and Russian."

"And do you speak them all without an accent?"

"Only the Soviet language," the girl answered with a sarcastic grin.

The stranger took me by the arm and explained that there was nothing to be afraid of. First, my father was highly trusted, and second I was being given a chance to serve the Great October Revolution.

Tatyana Alexeyevna wasn't afraid. Not then, at least. She understood very little, and that's why when that man began recruiting her as an agent, she didn't hesitate in the least.

"You go and work for your rainy October!—" I retorted, extricating myself from his embrace. He smiled condescendingly and followed me down the hallway. A few minutes later, the intelligence agent suggested that I take classes in typing and stenography. Things started to get interesting!

"What for?" I asked. He explained. His arguments seemed

convincing to me, and I agreed. So, there you go: A year after my
return to Moscow I'd become a correspondent-typist at the NKID.
"What's the NKID?"
"The People's Commissariat of Foreign Affairs—now it's the
MID. It's an amazing place! I think, at first, I even liked it.
Interesting people, fascinating work. A different world! It had
nothing in common with what I saw on the streets. I couldn't go
to Europe anymore, but here was an opportunity to be a little
closer to home."

Over time she earned their trust. Dozens of documents
passed through her hands every day. Coded messages, dispatches, foreign citizens' petitions. Letters from communists
abroad, translations, and appeals. She liked to repeat that it
was forever autumn in her office because papers were constantly falling onto her desk, like leaves from a tree.

I made a friend! Yes, a real friend. Pasha Azarov. He was only
one year younger than me. Very young, educated, and cheerful.
Like me, he'd been born abroad, not in London but in Genoa.
Pasha once said that we had a lot in common because it was the
Genovese who gave the English their flag with a red cross. We
were younger that most of our colleagues, and we had similar
memories. Milan, Verona, Lake Garda. The most amazing places
were preserved in our joint memory banks. I worked with docu-
ments, and Pasha was an assistant of the People's Commissar. I
liked him but understood that nothing could happen between
us—ours was like a friendship between two boys.

At that time, the NKID was located on Kuznetsky Bridge
Street.[1] During their lunch breaks the friends used to sit in a

---

[1] The name of this street is often rendered in historical texts and tourist
literature in its transliterated form, as Kuznetsky Most. However, because the
motif of bridges is so central to the novel—second only to crosses—we felt
that a translation of the street name was warranted. [Translators' note]

small square across from their office. English Leyland buses were driving around, and, as she watched them, Tatyana Alexeyevna imagined she was back in London.

We even made up a game: we'd close our eyes and invite each other to our hometowns. Azarov walked me through Genoa, and I walked with him down Tate Street, where Mark Twain and Oscar Wilde lived at some point, and where my home used to be.

My neighbor once again repeats the word "home," and I'm distracted. It's astonishing how familiar, worn-out words can suddenly acquire new meaning. From now on, when I say *home*, I'll be referring to a new place and another city. A former home and an emerging home, a home of childhood and a home of silence. Looking down at my full grocery bags, I think I need to call my mom and check on my daughter.

"You looked twice at your watch, Sasha. Aren't you interested in the slightest?"

"Oh no, it's not that. It's probably interesting . . . But, you know, I'm not going through the happiest time right now. The move, a different country. I'm feeling a little lost."

"Why did you move here?"

"I thought it would be better for my daughter."

"Is your daughter pretty?"

"I don't know, it's hard to say yet."

I was always an ugly child. Others would go through transformations—at eight you're an ugly duckling, but at ten you're a very decent-looking girl. But that wasn't my story. Just like the Soviet Union, I was consistent in my ugliness. I think I was twelve when Papa for some reason said, "Don't let it upset you, because you're very smart."

Really, men are heartless animals! If only someone had bothered to explain to them that one phrase like that can traumatize a girl for life. From that time on, I was always ashamed of myself. But I don't think my father really cared—he was building a new and perfect world. And while Papa was trying to establish relations with the West, I kept asking my nannies why he didn't love me. The old dears didn't answer; they just stroked my hair. But Papa wouldn't let it go. In Moscow, right before his death, he went back to that old conversation. "In reality, you know, you're very pretty. You just need to find a man who can see your beauty." My father could've stopped right there, but for some reason he continued, "You're like a constructivist building."

Yep, that's exactly what he said: "You, my dear, are like a constructivist house. Not everyone understands your beauty today, but believe me, years from now, everyone will come to admire you!"

Strangely enough, he didn't say anything about my functionality. But the funniest thing is that Papa was right—my husband was an architect. His name was Lyosha, or Alexey, just like Papa's. My husband used to say that it was love at first sight—from the moment he saw me for the first time in the square across from the NKID, he couldn't stop looking. That's ridiculous, but . . .

They met in the summer of 1934. It was the time of the slow foxtrot and of an approaching heat wave. By that time, several men had passed through her life without leaving a trace. Tatyana had never had any illusions about herself.

What did they used to say? Third rate does not a marriage make? That was about me. I realized they stayed the night because life is no picnic. Anyway, when Lyosha sat next to me to make my acquaintance, I thought he was a spy. No, I'm serious! By that time, I'd been living in Moscow for five years, working at the NKID, and constant fear had become a part of my life. If a stranger started talking to me, I decided he was a foreign agent. It all looked so strange. I'm sitting all by myself,

your typical ugly-duckling, and suddenly there he was—such a
beautiful man, and he wants to get to know me.

For the first few days, she didn't talk to him. Naturally. She
thought she was being tested. Lyosha was good at making
jokes, but Tatyana didn't even smile.

I remember asking Pasha Azarov if he thought it was possible
for someone to fall in love with me. A silly question, I know.
Moreover, it wasn't really the right question to ask. All the same,
Pasha patted me on the shoulder and asked: "What does he look
like?"
"Beautiful, intelligent, like a Swede."
"Maybe he's a spy?"
"I don't know, but it seems he's already gotten under my skin."
"You mean, you've already . . ."
"Don't be such a fool!"

Alexey was patient. He patiently endured all of Tatyana's
oddities. But she still treated him like an infiltrator. And with
every passing day, her suspicions only grew stronger. She
wouldn't surrender, and he wouldn't retreat.

Who would spend so much time on a plain Jane like me?
Moscow was filled with beauties, but he stuck to me like a leech.
Maybe he knew that I'd lived in the West? Maybe he wanted to
leave?

Every night in front of the mirror she went through dresses
and earrings, motives and reasons. With horror she tried to
guess when he'd disappear, but Lyosha didn't leave.

I was ready to believe in anything at all, just not in love. I
think I mentioned that I've always loved drawing, since I was a

*child. And, just imagine, Lyosha brought an easel on one of our
dates:*

"What's this?" I asked.

"It's for you."

"What for?"

"I saw you drawing on a piece of paper during lunch."

"Were you spying on me?"

"Silly, I just come here fairly often . . . on business."

"What kind of business?"

*"I'll tell you everything in due time. Let's go, I'll walk you
home." I don't know why, but I agreed. He looked so ridiculous
with that easel.*

"I also bought you some paint and brushes."

"What made you think that I'd accept all that?"

"If you don't take them, I'll give them to someone else."

"To another girl?"

He walked ahead of her and then turned around to face her,
smiling. A bag in one hand, an easel in the other. She looked at
him and understood that she already loved him and would love
him all her life.

*Being a troll, I should've been happy, but instead, I was act-
ing like some hard-to-get princess:*

"What did you want to tell me about your work?"

*"I wanted to tell you that I'm often here on Pompolit busi-
ness."*

"What's Pompolit?" I asked.

"Aid for Political Prisoners," my neighbor answered.
Before 1922 it was called the Moscow Committee of the
Political Red Cross. It's hard to believe now, but it existed in
the Soviet Union until 1938, when Yezhov officially closed it.
Lyosha didn't work for Pompolit but was helping them collect

money for convicts. He'd ask for money at poetry readings and music recitals."

"Wasn't it dangerous?"

"Not more dangerous than building bridges. A bridge that Lyosha's agency designed collapsed in 1936. All the workers and architects were sent to the Gulag. Alexey was lucky: a month before that happened, he'd been transferred to another project, and that saved him. Dumb luck. Had he been transferred, let's say, a week later, he would've been arrested, and everything would've turned out differently. But . . ."

"But what?"

"But as I told you—he wasn't arrested. Those were the years of the Great Terror and, therefore, years of great luck."

For a long time, especially because of Alexey's work, they believed there were still some people who could be helped. But by 1937, those hopes were gone. As a result of the pressure placed on Commissar Litvinov, purges began at the NKID as well. Of course, purges had happened before, but they assumed a mass scale only in 1937. Azarov, whom Tanya and Alexey visited often, lived at 5 Kuznetsky Bridge Street, very close to his office. In 1937, half of the apartments in his building were sealed off.

I'll never forget the mailboxes stuffed with envelopes. Who were those letters for? Who would ever read them?

As I climbed the stairs, I would count the number of sealed-off doors. One, two, three. That night in Pasha's living room, I whispered to Alexey, "Look, it's like we're in a mausoleum in the center of Moscow . . ."

In the 1980s, I learned that by 1939 at 5 Kuznetsky Bridge Street alone, seventeen people had been executed, including Pasha.

"Why didn't they arrest you?"

"Huh?"

"You said you lost your memory, not your hearing. I asked why they didn't arrest you."

"That's a very good question! What was in those people's heads?! Maybe they didn't want to? Or couldn't . . . First, I was on maternity leave in 1937 (after Lyosha avoided arrest, we decided to have a baby), and second . . . well, that's precisely what I wanted to tell you about . . ."

+

Beds—they were the only places where happy Soviet people could sometimes (if they were lucky enough not to live in a communal apartment) talk openly and freely among themselves, without fear. Covering his head with a blanket, Lyosha whispered, imitating Comrade Stalin's accent, "Everything here must be new! A new man brimming with a new heroism will perform new feats in the service of new days, new music, and new literature. We need new laws, new feelings, and new orders, so a new generation of Soviet people can freely enter a new epoch and begin producing completely new quality shit that has never been seen before!"

They began laughing and kissing, and for a moment they lived with the illusion that everything would work out one way or another . . .

You wouldn't believe it, but I liked Moscow. It was a terrible time, but somehow I believed the situation would change very soon.

"You're a hopeless optimist!" her husband would say, kissing her on the forehead. And so, what if she was? And why shouldn't she be? Can we really grasp our times? Can anyone really see the full of picture of the world? Was she an optimist? Yes, she was! She was happy. She'd just had a daughter, and her husband was wonderful. What else was there to dream of? Her little girl would laugh every time she saw her father, and

Tatyana knew that Lyosha was her soulmate. He was cheerful but modest, always ready to help, and calm. She liked the fact that he was always active and that, when possible, he preferred to be quiet.

Lyosha was that rare breed of man who sees love not as a word but as a deed. He was a man of action. He didn't talk much but did exactly as much as was needed for me to feel loved every minute. But I've digressed too much again . . . I think you asked why they didn't arrest me?

Initially, they assumed she was protected by her new surname—Pavkova. They thought that only foreigners—Poles, Germans, and Jews—were being arrested. But very soon, their theory proved false. The Russian, Masha Gavrina, from apartment 29 was arrested, and from apartment 31, Pyotr Andreevich Khrisanov. Nationality and occupation didn't matter anymore. Chauffeurs and executive assistants, diplomats and ordinary couriers suddenly stopped showing up at work.

I believe that, on the one hand, the investigators relied on material obtained from interrogations, while on the other, they realized that if they arrested everybody, the work of the ministry would be paralyzed. In a word, I don't know. I think they simply didn't get around to me. That happens. A machine's working and working, and then poof—there's a new task. It's important to understand that the main reason for the arrests was not enemies of the people, but conspiracies. When you chop wood, chips fly. It simply must be that, in that year, someone chopped down the tree a little higher than where I was.

Somehow, a few months after having her baby, Tatyana Alexeyevna returned to work. The place was so different! The

Chekists had really done a number on it. The majority of her new colleagues had absolutely no experience in diplomatic work.

"Where did they find them?" she thought. She had to explain the most elementary things to her new colleagues. Because of the constant purges, the consulates in Bulgaria, Spain, and many other countries were left without leadership.

You can't even imagine the chaos that descended on the commissariat. But even that wasn't enough for Stalin. Commissar Litvinov was relieved of his duties on May 3, 1939. Pasha was arrested the next morning. During one of our last nights together, we were sitting in his living room, and when I wanted to turn on the radio, he stopped me.

"Guys," he said quietly. "It feels like I live in this building all alone now . . ."

"All the more reason to turn on the radio!" Lyosha said, smiling. "There's nothing to worry about. Asya doesn't mind music, and your neighbors won't complain . . ."

"That's exactly why I don't want to play music . . ."

I think Pasha foresaw his arrest. Place of birth? The city of Genoa. Got it. A red cross over your fate.

That night, Pasha gave us an issue of the children's magazine Murzilka. Back home sitting next to Asya's crib, Lyosha read her a poem by Agniya Barto:

Near Stone Bridge in Moscow,
Where the Moscow River flows,
Near Stone Bridge in Moscow,
A narrow street unfolds.

The traffic there caused such delay,
The drivers were enraged,
"That house is clearly in the way,"
The local gendarme said.

Syoma was away at camp—
And living in a tent,
Until he took the train back home,
To Moscow Syoma went.

But at that old familiar place,
Syoma stood in total fear:
Of his old house, there was no trace!
His eyes filled up with tears.

His house, which once had stood right there,
Right on that very spot,
Had now completely disappeared!
Poor Syoma was distraught!

"Where is building number four?"
Cried Syoma in alarm.
"I cannot see it anymore!"
Syoma said to the gendarme.

"I'm now back from the Crimea,
With no home to shelter me!
Where is that big gray house of mine
Where Mama used to be?"

The gendarme then explained to him:
"Your journey's incomplete.
It was decreed to take your home
And move it down the street.

Take a look around the corner—
You'll find your old house there."
"Have I gone completely mad?

Syoma whispered in despair.

It seems that you have told me
Houses can in fact be moved?
Syoma went in search of neighbors
Who had surely disapproved:

"We've been moving, Syoma, calmly,
Moving now for ten days straight,
Moving very, very slowly,
So as not to break a plate.

Not a vase and not a lightbulb
Has been broken as of yet."
"Is there nothing," marveled Syoma,
"Moving houses won't upset."

Then in summer to the country
We'll travel in this house!
But when our neighbors stopping by
Find nothing, won't they grouse?

I just cannot do my homework,
I'll tell all my teachers then:
"My textbooks in the house have gone,
I don't know where, I don't know when."

Together with the house we'll go
Into the woods to roam.
We'll wander with the house in tow
And then return—but there's no home.

Our house has gone to Leningrad
To see the big parade,

But will return tomorrow morn.
It will return, or so it said.

Before it left, the house decreed:
"Wait here beside the door,
And do not try to follow me,
It's my day off to explore."

But Syoma, he had had enough,
"A house can't go its merry way!"
The owner of the house is king,
Over all he must hold sway.

So, on the sea or in the sky,
We can now just sail away,
Or if we wish—
We'll move a house
If it is in the way![2]

Of course, Barto's poem was about relocating an apartment building on Serafimovich Street, not about the thousands of arrests, but I couldn't hold back my tears. You know, Sasha, sometimes I think that if that night we had made dots on a map of Moscow to mark all the arrests, the city would have looked like a sieve . . .

I look through the window: the sky's getting dark. Tatyana Alexeyevna turns toward her paintings and, as if going through the card catalogue of her memory, arranges the canvases.

"Here, I want to show you something . . ." she says as she takes one of the paintings and holds it up. A night train cuts

---

[2] All translations of Russian poetry and songs are by Brian James Baer, unless otherwise indicated. [Translators' note]

diagonally across the ground. The colors are black and blue. These cars are for carrying freight, not passengers. There's shadow and darkness. Only the first car emits a yellow glow. The locomotive is small and narrow while the canvas is huge. I expect my neighbor to start talking about this painting, but Tatyana Alexeyevna suddenly puts the canvas down and, nodding to herself, goes over to a small table. She removes an album from its cover, then turns on the record player.

"I can't remember now when I heard this for the first time. One night, Lyosha invited me to the Philharmonic. He had to meet someone there on Pompolit business and decided to take me with him. From the very first chords, I forgot about everything. The Fifth Symphony. Tchaikovsky. For me, this piece of music could replace any textbook. Our entire history is in this one symphony. If any instrument can be considered the voice of this country, then, of course, it's the clarinet in the opening. Every time I listen to the first movement, I imagine that Tchaikovsky wrote it about me. The anxious overture, tiny glimmers of hope, and the triumph of death descending into a desolate spring. A prelude of alarm, drama in a minor key. The cautious steps of an ordinary fate in total darkness. I think Tchaikovsky, without even realizing it, wrote a hymn to fatalism and the approaching disaster. After several minutes you realize, of course, that Tchaikovsky wrote the finale in a major key—there is light and hope in Tchaikovsky's Fifth. Maybe it's so . . . maybe it's true for someone, but not for me. My story ended in the first movement . . ."

"May I ask you a question?"

"Of course. Can I make you some tea?"

"No, thanks, I'll really need to be going soon. Need to get up early tomorrow—they'll be delivering my furniture and the kitchen cabinets."

"So, do you want black or green?"

"I guess black."

"What did you want to ask?"

"I've always been interested in people who hold positions like yours, people who work in the Ministry. You knew everything back then, didn't you?"

"What do you mean?" my neighbor asked, rummaging around in a drawer.

"I'm talking about the war. You knew there'd be war, didn't you?"

"With Germany?"

"Yes."

"Before September of 1939, there was a possibility, but after the Molotov–Ribbentrop Pact, we became almost friends. When Hitler wished Stalin a happy birthday, Stalin referred to their 'friendship cemented in blood.' I was positive there'd be no war."

"And why was that?"

"First, Germany didn't have the capability yet; second, I was personally sending a list of books that needed to be destroyed to all our consulates in Europe. All those books were being confiscated for the sole reason that they contained negative remarks about the Nazi party and Hitler. I'd also been sending out information about German communists who were extradited to Germany. Not bad, huh? The Soviet Union sent back communists for the fascists to torture! I don't remember if I told you that, at the time, the NKID was on Kuznetsky Bridge Street . . ."

"Yes, you did."

"There was a small book shop and a printing press squeezed onto the first floor of our building. So, all the books containing some unfavorable mention of Hitler were confiscated from there too, from the very center of Moscow. In November of 1939, I was sitting at my desk typing out Molotov's speech, which contained some absolutely shocking things:

THE IDEOLOGY OF HITLERISM, AS WELL AS ANY OTHER IDEOLOGICAL SYSTEM, CAN BE ACCEPTED OR REFUSED—THIS IS A MATTER OF POLITICAL BELIEF. BUT ANY PERSON SHOULD UNDERSTAND THAT YOU CAN NEITHER DESTROY IDEOLOGY BY FORCE NOR FINISH IT OFF BY WAR. HENCE IT IS NOT ONLY SENSELESS BUT ALSO CRIMINAL TO FIGHT SUCH A WAR, OR AS THEY CALL IT, A WAR FOR THE 'DESTRUCTION OF HITLERISM,' WHICH THEY DISGUISE WITH THE FALSE FLAG OF FIGHTING FOR 'DEMOCRACY.'

"Charming, isn't it? It was a crime to fight fascism! Our diplomats learned this lesson well, and when the German army entered Paris, they came out to greet the fascist troops. An even more absurd thing happened with our ambassador in France. After the French declared Iakov Surits persona non-grata, Nikolay Nikolayevich Ivanov was appointed *chargé d'affaires* to our consulate in Paris. Nikolay Nikolayevich was a direct man, a true communist, and an anti-fascist. When talking about Hitler, he never minced words, and, eventually, he had to pay for that. Once they found out this official representative was overstepping his bounds, Moscow recalled him and immediately arrested him. Ivanov got five years for 'anti-German sentiment.' And do you know when? In September of 1941! The fascist armies were approaching Moscow, and we were prosecuting our diplomats for saying bad things about Hitler."

"That's ridiculous. Does that mean you didn't suspect the catastrophe that was approaching?"

"Catastrophe? Are people capable of spotting a tragedy before it strikes? My daughter was growing up, I had a wonderful husband. The Second World War? We mistakenly thought that after the horror of the First, nothing like that could possibly happen again. They were constantly brainwashing us by repeating that Russia was surrounded by enemies: Poland, Finland, Japan; but I felt the real danger was lurking here, in Moscow. When Pasha's picture was taken down from the wall of honor in our office, I understood that, for me, the real danger would come from the NKVD, not from some Germans. In 1941, we began receiving one message after another about a possible invasion by Germany, but soon there were so many of those messages that we stopped paying any attention to them. I remember very well the twenty-second of June. I had the night shift. We got a call from the German Embassy requesting an urgent meeting with Molotov. At that moment, he was with Stalin, so we contacted the Kremlin, arranged a visit, and called the Germans back. A few hours after the bombing had begun, the German Ambassador Schulenburg met with Molotov in the Kremlin."

"And did you know what they were talking about?"

"Of course! The very next morning Molotov's assistant Gostev recounted everything to us."

"And what did he tell you?"

"Nothing special. According to him, Schulenburg apologized, claiming that he hadn't known anything himself, that for many years he'd personally been working to establish cooperation between our two countries. He then read us the now famous German communiqué: 'In view of the steadily increasing threat presented to Germany's Eastern border as a result of the massive concentration and training of Red Army forces, the German government feels compelled to undertake immediate counter-measures.' 'And what do you think these words mean?' Molotov asked in surprise. 'In my opinion, this is war,' Schulenberg answered.

"Gostev told us that Molotov then tried to clarify the situation. He said that there was no unusual concentration of Red Army forces on the German border. These were only regular maneuvers that take place every year. Molotov was in total shock and kept saying that he didn't quite understand what the problem was since the German government had never registered any complaints. Schulenberg could only answer that he didn't have anything to add."

"And that's it?! So simple? They were planning to slaughter half of Europe, and the conversation ended right there?"

"What else was there to say? But their conversation, of course, wasn't finished. After that, they only discussed logistical questions. Schulenberg didn't have any instructions on how to evacuate the Embassy or the headquarters of various German companies, so he asked Soviet authorities to cooperate in providing safe passage for German citizens. Schulenberg explained that, with Romania and Finland entering the war alongside Germany, it was impossible to evacuate German citizens across the Western border. And so, the German Ambassador suggested they go through Iran. Molotov agreed to that and expressed the hope that Soviet organizations in Germany would not face any obstacles from the German government. With that, they departed. Ah no, wait! I recall that at the end of their meeting Molotov asked again, 'Why did Germany sign the Treaty of Non-Aggression if it was so easy to break?'"

"And how did Schulenberg respond to that?"

"Schulenberg said that there was no escaping fate . . ."

+

T atyana Alexeyevna didn't go home on June 23, 1941. After listening to Gostev, she went back to her desk and began typing the Red Cross telegram that had just been translated from the French:

> FROM GENEVA, 23 JUNE 1941
> TO HIS EXCELLENCY
> PEOPLE'S COMMISSAR OF FOREIGN AFFAIRS
> MOSCOW
>
> STRIVING TO ADEQUATELY FULFILL ITS HUMANITARIAN MISSION, THE INTERNATIONAL COMMITTEE OF THE RED CROSS OFFERS TO THE USSR GOVERNMENT ITS COOPERATION IN CASES WHEN SUCH MEDIATION, IN ACCORDANCE WITH THE RED CROSS'S PRINCIPLES, COULD BE OF ANY USE, ESPECIALLY THE COLLECTION AND EXCHANGE OF INFORMATION REGARDING THE INJURED AND IMPRISONED ACCORDING TO THE PROTOCOL THAT IS CURRENTLY IN EFFECT WITH THE ASSISTANCE OF THE CENTRAL AGENCY OF THE INTERNATIONAL PRISONERS-OF-WAR COMMITTEE FOR ALL COUNTRIES INVOLVED.
> THE INTERNATIONAL COMMITTEE OF THE RED CROSS PROPOSES THE FOLLOWING ACTION: THAT THE USSR GOVERNMENT ORDER THE COMPILATION OF LISTS OF HEALTHY AND INJURED PRISONERS OF WAR, INDICATING SURNAME, FIRST NAME, MILITARY RANK, PLACE OF IMPRISONMENT, PHYSICAL CONDITION, AND IF POSSIBLE, FATHER'S NAME AND PLACE OF

BIRTH. THE SAME INFORMATION SHOULD BE PROVIDED FOR THE DECEASED. ALL THIS INFORMATION WILL BE USED FOR THE FOLLOWING PURPOSES:

TO BE PASSED ALONG TO THE OPPOSING SIDES;

TO PROVIDE INFORMATION TO FAMILIES THAT CONTACT THE INTERNATIONAL COMMITTEE OF THE RED CROSS.

TO EXPEDITE THE SUBMISSION OF ALL THE INFORMATION COLLECTED, WE ARE EXPLORING THE POSSIBILITY OF ORGANIZING A LOCAL BRANCH IN THE MOST GEOGRAPHICALLY SUITABLE LOCATION. THE SAME PROPOSITION IS BEING EXTENDED TO THE GOVERNMENTS OF GERMANY, FINLAND, AND ROMANIA.

WE ASSUME THAT THE NON-PARTICIPATION OF THE USSR IN THE 1929 GENEVA CONVENTION ON THE TREATMENT OF PRISONERS OF WAR WILL NOT INTERFERE WITH THE PROPOSITIONS OUTLINED ABOVE IF THEY ARE ACCEPTED BY BOTH PARTIES INVOLVED IN THE CONFLICT.

IN ANTICIPATION OF YOUR EXCELLENCY'S REPLY, WE SEND YOU OUR HIGHEST REGARDS.

MAX HUBER
INTERNATIONAL COMMITTEE OF THE RED CROSS

In the first days of the war, she didn't feel a sense of catastrophe. Tatyana sincerely believed that the conflict would be over at any moment. When you type international documents by the hour, when your desk is buried under papers, and people are buzzing around you like bees, you begin to feel that the problem will be resolved with the greatest possible speed.

Tatyana Alexeyevna understood that, despite the speed of the Germans' advance, the USSR was urgently attempting through different channels to reach an agreement with Germany. It was proposed to Hitler that he pause, stop the attack, and decide what territory he wanted to take.

*I don't think we were really planning to give Germany
Ukraine or Belorussia, but we needed time to regroup our military, so our agents were meeting with their German counter-
parts and passing along the most obvious hints that they were
willing to sit down at the negotiating table. I was sure these
efforts would bear fruit. The war will end, surely it will end, I
thought as I took my daughter to kindergarten. A week passed,
then another, but I still naively believed that the conflict would
end soon. Only at the end of August, when Lyosha left for the
Southern front, did I realize that something truly terrible had
happened . . .*

I take a sip of tea. It's hot, strong, and sweet. My neighbor
is smiling. Again, I look at my watch but decide to stay.

*In a month, I received the first letters. Two at once. Lyosha's
letters didn't tell me anything. He didn't want to worry me. I
admired my husband. He was there, in the thick of it, but his only
concern was to not frighten me. He was totally calm. He wrote
about silly things, trying to reassure me. He said that the weather
was nice, and the food was good. He told me that he was serving
beside a talented musician, and that they had recently found a
piano in an abandoned school, and his comrade-in-arms played
him Liszt's Hungarian Rhapsody. He said that in his division there
were many simple Russians who, it seemed, didn't always share
his political views, but it didn't matter anymore—people had
united against the enemy and that was the most important thing.*

Tatyana Alexeyevna knew that her husband was destroying
bridges, and this gave her some hope. "At the very least," she
mistakenly reasoned, "he's not on the front line. When retreat-
ing, they'll try to cut off all the routes from the Germans ahead
of time, and so Lyosha shouldn't have to face the enemy . . ."

I remember very well the wide eyes of the salesgirl in the music shop. Astonishment. Annoyance and confusion. There was regret and anger in that woman's eyes:

"Gosh, there's a war, but they come to buy music! What's wrong with these people? Do you really want Liszt's Hungarian Rhapsody? Why that piece, exactly? Why are you buying music at such a time? Are you trying to remain human and continue a normal life? Are you trying not to notice the tragedy? You want to go home, kick off your shoes, and turn on some music?"

No, she didn't want to do that. Tatyana Alexeyevna just wanted to feel closer to her husband. She wanted to understand how he was really doing. Now for the first time when listening to Liszt, she heard bombs exploding in the chords. She no longer heard merriment and jokes but the horror she would soon be living through. In Liszt's playful passages, which used to make her smile, Tatyana Alexeyevna now heard only the irrational and the absurd, the slapstick comedy and diabolic grotesquery of the beginnings of war.

Her apprehension grew stronger in the middle of October. There were no more letters from Alexey, but after some leaked gossip from the front, Moscow was fleeing.

Those four days when the capital realized that the fascists were very close were filled with horror and dread; everyone naturally lost their minds. The instinct for self-preservation rose up in its purest form. For the first time in history, the metro was closed. This seemed like the last shoe to drop. This was a country of weathervanes, the citizens of which had learned during all the years of lies to discern the slightest hint that something bad was going to happen. They decided that the closing of the metro was a sign. Staraya Square emptied; money disappeared. The capital's most important buildings were readied for potential bombings. Tatyana Alexeyevna was in her office when some guy started walking around her desk contemplating

where to put the explosives. Along with other government com-
missariats, the NKID would be evacuated to the city of
Kuybyshev, but Molotov's secretariat had to stay in Moscow.

"What will happen to us?"

"Everything will be fine, don't worry! They say Zhukov
promised we'd be able to ride this out!"

"Will we really?"

"Definitely!"

Moscow wasn't as trusting as Tanya; its residents weren't
buying any promises. Over the next four days people left in
trucks, cars, and horse-drawn transports. At the sight of any
slow-moving truck, men would help their wives and children
get inside. The people who were lucky enough to make it
inside the vehicle would defend their places with suitcases and
duffle bags. Neither the friendship of Soviet peoples nor the
ideals of the October Revolution could withstand the survival
instinct, and when it came to spontaneous evacuation, people
went wild and abandoned all sentiment.

"Take your hands off me, asshole! Get out of here! I'll kill
you, bitch!"

For a long time, the Party had been telling people that
there were no privileged classes in the USSR. And for decades
foreign writers and philosophers, whose services Tanya's
father had so painstakingly employed, were passing this information to the West, but in October of 1941 there was no
doubt—the privileged were leaving the capital. When ordinary people heard about this, they took to the streets and
began blockading all the exits out of Moscow. Angry Russian
men gathered in crowds and blocked traffic, attacking any
vehicle that was trying to leave the city. They'd take money
from the well-off and beat them up, then push their vehicles
into a ditch. In Moscow, crowds vandalized store windows,
while the true Stalinists, in fear of the approaching enemy,

were burning documents. The leader's most faithful servants demanded private train cars to evacuate their vases, sofas, and paintings . . .

I told you already that I received only two letters from my husband. Then there was silence. I wasn't worried at first—there were interruptions like that even at work. I tried to be strong. My husband was fighting the war and I had to be worthy of him. Hardship was everywhere, but we were used to it; we were used to it because tragedy had become the norm.

+

E very day on her way home from work, Tatyana Alexeyevna passed Azarov's apartment building. She wanted to climb the familiar stairs and ring the bell, but she knew her friend wouldn't open his door. She hadn't heard anything about him for two years. At the NKID it was rumored that there had been an investigation and that Pasha would be released any day now. But she couldn't help thinking, "What kind of investigation lasts for seven hundred days?"

In 1941, they worked without any days off. After finishing one document, Tatyana Alexeyevna would immediately start on the next. Ambassadors' reports and outcomes of negotiations, tearful letters to Comrade Stalin, and dispatches from foreign countries. From the first days of the war, the International Red Cross tried to establish relations with the Soviet Union, but, unfortunately, nothing came of it. In Geneva, they proposed that prisoners of war be exchanged and, to whatever extent possible, injured combatants helped. However, it immediately became clear that the Soviet Union wasn't interested in those efforts. The NKID typically "underreacted" or, more often, simply didn't respond to the letters from Switzerland.

TELEGRAM

FROM GENEVA
20 OCTOBER 1941

PEOPLE'S COMMISSAR OF
FOREIGN AFFAIRS
MOSCOW

WE WOULD LIKE TO INFORM YOU THAT WE HAVE
RECEIVED THE LIST OF THE 2,894 SOVIET PRISONERS OF WAR
IN ROMANIA, WHICH WE WILL PASS ON TO YOU THROUGH
OUR DELEGATION IN ANKARA. WE WOULD ALSO LIKE TO
INFORM YOU THAT THE GOVERNMENT OF ROMANIA HAS COM-
MUNICATED TO US THEIR DECISION TO WITHHOLD SENDING
ANY FUTURE LISTS UNTIL THEY RECEIVE THE NAMES OF
ROMANIAN PRISONERS OF WAR IN THE USSR.

INTERNATIONAL RED CROSS

*With time I learned from incoming correspondence that our
bosses wrote the same recommendation on almost all the letters
from the Red Cross:*
"Do not respond."

Geneva asked Moscow to issue visas for two of their representatives, but those requests were ignored. The Red Cross
made the request again and again, but the NKID kept silent,
on orders from above.

*This ordeal with prisoners of war was only a distraction for
us. The NKID had more important business to attend to. Meanwhile they kept telling us that a brave soldier cannot be captured.
And if a soldier surrendered, then he was a coward. As strange
as it may be, I heard this most often from men here, in Moscow.
A Soviet soldier must fight until his last drop of blood. Period.
Next paragraph.*

At the beginning of the winter of 1941, the Red Cross sent
the promised list of Soviet prisoners of war from the Romanian

front. When that document appeared on Tatyana Alexeyevna's desk, the paper sent shivers up and down her spine.

I don't know why, but I decided to check if our last name was on the list. Cautiously, trying not to attract attention, I took the index cards attached to the list and began reading the prisoners' names. The Romanians didn't bother to alphabetize them, so I had to read the names and surnames several times before I finally came across the name of my husband . . .

There was no doubt—everything matched: the initials, the rank, and the year of birth. She almost passed out. This was probably how someone who has run to the top of Mont Blanc feels. Oxygen deficiency or something like that.

I don't know how to describe it, but I felt like I was going to die right there.

With trembling hands, she put the cards aside, carefully pushed her chair back, and left the office. Her legs were like rubber; her head was spinning. On the street she almost got hit by a bus. "Watch where you're going!" some woman shouted, letting out a cloud of hot air.

I don't remember how, but I made it to a little park and fell onto a bench covered with snow. In my work shoes I was just like a cow on ice. It was cold outside, but I didn't feel a thing.

She was shaking from the shock, not from the cold. Covering her mouth with her hand, she tried to calm down.
"He's alive! Alive! Alive!" she whispered.
A momentary death. A pause. Snow was falling on Moscow, but, for her, time had stopped. Silence hung over the Earth. Quiet. As if someone had turned off the sound. A healing

emptiness. Tatyana Alexeyevna learned that her husband was wounded, but he was alive . . .

Wounded but alive.

She should have returned immediately to the office, but she couldn't move.

You can't even imagine what was happening inside me!

"Pasha, Pasha, where are you now, Pasha? I need to talk to you right now. I need your advice! Lyosha is a prisoner of war. Can you imagine that? Yes, Lyosha is a prisoner of war! Yes, Lyosha is a POW. Yes, captured by the Romanians. Where? I don't know. No, don't worry, I won't tell anybody."

Tatyana Alexeyevna tried unsuccessfully to calm herself down and to put her thoughts in order. Happiness? Not at all! At that moment she felt anything but happiness:

First: Lyosha is alive.

Second: Lyosha is in a POW camp. Why is he a POW? How is he doing? How is he being treated there? Is everything all right with him? He's badly wounded . . . What could that mean? A bullet? An explosion? A bayonet? Maybe he lost a limb? In any case, he's alive right now, and that's the most important thing! They'll want to exchange him, so he'll be home very soon! I'll embrace him, and we'll be together again! Lyosha, Asya, and me . . .

Second: No, the second thing is that Lyosha is in a POW camp.

Third: Lyosha is in a POW camp and, therefore, I shouldn't talk about it. Yes, tell no one!

"But why?"

"Why what?"

"Why couldn't you tell anyone that your husband was a POW?"

"Because I remembered very well Order № 270, which was published in August in all the newspapers:

COMMANDERS AND POLITICAL OFFICERS WHO TEAR OFF THEIR INSIGNIA AND DESERT TO THE REAR OR SURRENDER TO THE ENEMY DURING COMBAT SHALL BE CONSIDERED MALICIOUS DESERTERS WHOSE FAMILIES ARE SUBJECT TO ARREST AS A FAMILY FOR THE VIOLATION OF THEIR OATH AND BETRAYAL OF THEIR HOMELAND."

In reality, things were even more complicated. Tatyana Alexeyevna worked at the NKID and so was covered by a special order. According to that order, in special cases, the families of POW soldiers could not only be exiled for fifteen years but also executed by a firing squad. That was her situation.

I hope you remember what kind of papers were passing across my desk, and where I was born . . .

She was trapped. In a single moment her life had been turned upside down. It was a steel-jaw leghold trap beautifully designed by fate. Alexey had been captured. Her husband was now an enemy of the people, and, therefore, automatically, she too became an enemy of the people.

"I have to go! I need to get back to work now!" Tatyana Alexeyevna kept telling herself, and finally got up from the bench. Going back to the NKID, she thought that she must take action. It's amazing how fast a human mind can process information—a million combinations in a second. Instantaneous realization. In spite of the fog that was covering her eyes, her brain worked brilliantly. She was calculating all the possible combinations as if she were the greatest chess player in the world . . .

Don't think that I'm trying to come up with excuses. No! I assume responsibility for everything I'm guilty of! But there's another thing that's interesting here. What surprises me the most is how fast, literally in a moment, morality can be shut down. Poof! Dehumanization takes only a second.

How many times at parties, after a drink or two, have we argued with our friends about what steps we would have taken?

No, I'd never do anything like that! Even under the threat of death, I'd never act like that! Betrayal? What are you talking about? Make a false accusation? Never! Everything has its limits, don't you think? What about morality? And what about honor? Did you hear that X and Y wrote a denunciation? Would I write such a thing? Of course, not! Never! Slander another person? Nonsense! I wouldn't do something like that even under torture. What if my children's lives depended on it? Nothing could make me stop being human!

Fat chance! In reality, nothing is ever that simple. If humans have really accomplished anything, it's the ability to negotiate with their own conscience.

Climbing up the steps, she was tapping her teeth with her index finger as if it were a little shaking hammer:

Think, think, think . . . The Red Cross petition is typed in French. The POW's last names are written in Latin letters. If someone at work reads this list . . . If someone notices, compares, and realizes that my husband is on that list . . . But that's very unlikely. No one in the office will do that—there are too many other things to deal with. Who would have any interest in those surnames? There are almost three thousand people on the list! Who would read through all those? The women in our office? But I don't think they have anyone at the front. Only Lena, it seems, had a husband, but he was killed in early fall. Then my colleagues should be no problem . . . Okay, calm down, don't worry . . . Easy, easy, let's keep going . . . Most likely no one will notice anything here, but at the NKVD . . . the NKVD is a totally different thing . . . Now I'll translate the document and give it to my boss. In a few days the list will be sent to the NKVD, and those comrades won't wait, they'll act without hesitation. They're not planning to go to the front—they have their own sacred war to fight here. The more people they imprison, the more accolades they receive. I think only the translated list will be sent to the NKVD. What if I make a typo? What if I change only one syllable in the surname? I'm sure no one will cross-check the lists. If I change only one of the letters of his initials, they'll look for another man . . . Only which syllable should I change in the surname Pavkov? Damn it, Lyosha, why do you have a name like that! No, I can't change a syllable there. Plus, if they can't find this person or they figure out that something is off, they'll send a second request and demand the originals, and then they'll find out everything. I wonder if we have to provide them with the originals. Who would know that? Who can I ask? No, I'd better not ask anyone about it, definitely not! Maybe it would be better just to cross out Lyosha's name altogether? But then the total number of POWs wouldn't match. On the one hand, they wouldn't know about it at the NKVD and would search for one wife less; on the other hand, comparing the number of soldiers can be done only here, in our office . . .

And so, she decided to save her husband and herself, but she still couldn't figure out how to do it. As she entered the office, she tried to collect her thoughts and return to her desk as if nothing had happened. First, she decided to check the document one more time.

What if it was just my imagination? What if it wasn't my husband on that list?

But no, everything was correct. It was indeed Alexey in that Romanian POW camp.

There was no time for deliberation. A solution must be found immediately. First, she translated the Red Cross cover letter, then the list of names. Tatyana typically dealt with such documents much faster, but here an obvious weight was slowing her down. Two and a half hours later, she finally reached him, she reached Lyosha's name.

What if they don't look for anyone? It's a war after all . . . Do we even have the time to do battle with our own citizens? Why would they prosecute us when the enemy is advancing? Okay, so . . . calm down . . . think . . . think . . . think objectively . . . War is war, but these guys have other things to do . . . Let's imagine that the list reaches them after all . . . Then it follows that the list would need to be altered . . . But if they realize that I altered the document, then without a doubt, they'll throw me in front of a firing squad. Maybe I should tell them everything myself? What if I show up and give a heartfelt confession? Maybe they wouldn't touch me then? It might even be possible to come to some agreement with them. They can use me as an example. They'll say, "Look here—she's a real communist! She learned that her husband had become an enemy of the people and she denounced him!" It's good propaganda, isn't it? If I make a deal with my conscience, then at least I'll be able to take care of Asya. I can say that I don't want to know this enemy of the people. Yes, that's exactly what I'll tell them, "Comrades, forgive my family!" Maybe I should file for divorce? Draw up the document immediately before anything gets exposed? I'm sure Lyosha would understand. I'm doing it to save Asya, not just myself. No doubt—he would do the same. Lyosha loves me . . . He wouldn't condemn us . . . But wait, it can't be . . . As soon as they learn that a husband of an employee who has access to secret documents has gone over to the enemy's side, they'll arrest me in a second. Damn . . . Damn . . . Damn . . .

*

"Why did you stop talking?"

"Ah?"

"I'm asking why you stopped talking? What did you do?"

"What do you mean?"

"What did you do with the document?"

"Uh . . . I don't recall . . ."

"What do you mean you don't recall? You've been telling me every last detail!"

"I'm just joking, Sasha, just joking. Funny, isn't it? When else do I have the chance to joke if not now? It's a funny story, right? You turn on the TV and they show you people who are supposedly nostalgic for those times. Many people can't live without fear. What did I do, you ask? What could I do? What would you have done in my place?"

"I don't know, it's hard for me to answer right away."

"Hard to answer right away. It was hard for me too. Just that morning, I was an ordinary Soviet woman without any inner conflicts. My conscience was clear. I'd always lived an honest life, never lied to anyone, and never betrayed anyone. Now, at noon on that same gray, cold day, my fate presented me with a problem that was not so easy to solve. How does the song go? 'What to do then? What to do . . . Let go or forget, I can't do it, no I can't . . .'"

"That song isn't about that."

"It's not about that . . . yes . . . you're right . . . What did I do? I did something that I've regretted all my life . . ."

+

S he was sitting at her desk looking at her husband's name. There was his name on the Romanian list, but it wasn't yet in the translated Russian document. The time had come to act. To add her husband to the Russian list would allow her to keep a clear conscience, but it would be a risk that could endanger not only herself but her daughter as well. And if she didn't include his name? In that case, there was a chance of avoiding arrest, but Tatyana Alexeyevna was afraid the NKVD would notice.

"Imagine a person playing chess with himself and recording all the moves. There's no one in the room, and while playing black, you steal a single white pawn from the board. What would you do? Would you record the theft? How else could it have happened? There was a pawn there, and, suddenly, it's missing. Maybe no one would even notice? Who cares about an ordinary game of chess?"

"So, what did you do?"

"What did I do? What did I do? I put another man in danger . . ."

"But how?"

"Very simply. I put one chess piece on two squares."

When it was Alexey's turn, Tatyana typed the name from the previous line a second time. Now there was one man, the same soldier, under numbers 567 and 568, but it wasn't Lyosha, her husband. Lyosha's last name, Pavkov, should've followed Pavkin, but by typing the name of the unknown soldier twice, Tatyana Alexeyevna was able to remove her husband's name from the list.

My neighbor stops her story. After taking a sip of her tea, she glances in my direction:

"I know what you're thinking now, 'How could she do that? Why didn't she cross out other names? Why did she rescue only herself? Why didn't she rewrite the whole list?' Many years later I thought I should actually have done that. Maybe I should've misspelled all two thousand names. In that case, I would've confused the snoopers for some time, although they would've figured it out very soon and found me along with all the others. So, it wouldn't have made any sense and wouldn't have been heroic at all.

"Besides, what's the point talking about it now? I didn't do it anyway. Was I afraid? I was, certainly. I'm not even trying to redeem myself. On that day I acted like a coward, I understand that, but believe me, life has punished me pretty harshly . . ."

She didn't know who that soldier was. She didn't have a clue. Tatyana Alexeyevna only knew that he was another Soviet citizen, just like her husband; another wounded soldier but with one difference—his name was one line above her husband's on that list, and now his name was listed twice. That's it! That truly was the end of the story. She didn't know that guy but sent two packs of hounds to sniff out his family's tracks.

"I decided that the NKVD would interpret the repeated name as a regular typing error. Moreover, if they were really going to arrest all the wives, they'd have an enormous task on their hands—finding and arresting several thousand women. It was unlikely, I reasoned, that those comrades would bother with such an insignificant detail as one human life . . ."

After submitting the documents, she promised herself she'd go on living her usual life. "Nothing has happened," she kept repeating. "Not a single thing has happened." It was just a typing error. More likely than not, a typist was inattentive and typed this name twice. Someone should call the NKID and tell them to spank the typist.

"I was sure I could handle it. I believed that I had enough strength, and that the papers that kept falling on my desk would distract me. Once I finished the list, I turned it in. And the Russian version, which according to my prognosis was to be sent to the NKVD, no longer contained Alexey's name."

+

THE INTERNATIONAL COMMITTEE OF THE RED CROSS WITH
DEEPEST CONDOLENCES INFORMS YOU THAT

RED ARMY SOLDIER ANTON BESSONOV, BORN 1925, WAS BADLY
WOUNDED ON THE FINNISH FRONT AND, AFTER BEING TAKEN
FROM THE BATTLEFIELD BY FINNISH SOLDIERS, WAS TRANS-
PORTED TO FINNISH MILITARY FIELD HOSPITAL 58, WHERE,
DESPITE ALL MEDICAL EFFORTS TO SAVE HIS LIFE, HE SUCCUMBED
TO HIS INJURIES AND PASSED AWAY ON 9 DECEMBER 1941.
THIS INFORMATION WAS OBTAINED FROM THE DECEASED SOLDIER'S
COMRADES, WHO WERE TREATED AT THE SAME FIELD HOSPITAL.
ACCORDING TO THE LAST WISH OF THE DECEASED, WE ASK YOU
TO PASS THIS SAD INFORMATION ON TO MRS. BESSONOV, WHO
RESIDES IN THE VILLAGE OF YEMERENO IN THE KALININ
REGION. MRS. BESSONOV'S FIRST NAME AND HER RELATION TO
THE DECEASED SOLDIER ARE UNKNOWN.
WE THANK YOU IN ADVANCE FOR YOUR COURTESY. PLEASE
ACCEPT OUR ASSURANCES OF THE UTMOST RESPECT.
INTERNATIONAL COMMITTEE OF THE RED CROSS

THE INTERNATIONAL COMMITTEE OF THE RED CROSS
INFORMS YOU THAT THE RED ARMY SOLDIER:

DMITRY SEMYONOVICH KURILENKO

DIED ON 14 NOVEMBER 1941 IN THE VICINITY OF GORLOVKA, UKRAINE, IN THE DIRECTION OF NIKITOVKA. THE SOLDIER WAS BURIED TO THE RIGHT OF THE PAVED ROAD THAT LEADS FROM GORLOVKA TO NIKITOVKA, PAST THE BRIDGE OVER THE RAILROAD TRACKS.

THIS INFORMATION WAS RECEIVED FROM THE ITALIAN RED CROSS.

THE FIRST NAMES AND SURNAMES OF THE DECEASED'S RELATIVES ARE NOT INDICATED.

PLEASE ACCEPT OUR ASSURANCES OF THE OUTMOST RESPECT.

INTERNATIONAL COMMITTEE OF THE RED CROSS
CENTRAL AGENCY OF POW AFFAIRS
BRUNO DE LOEFF

The Red Cross kept sending telegrams. Every day, with great agitation, Tatyana Alexeyevna awaited the letters from Geneva. As she read the stories of fallen soldiers, she realized that the next document might be a notification of her husband's death.

"The Red Cross, with sincere regret, informs you that Red Army soldier . . ." No, luckily, not killed, luckily only wounded, luckily not him but someone else . . .

Weeks passed. We received a large number of new telegrams, but I didn't learn anything more about Alexey. Nothing new. Seriously wounded. He was on one list but excluded from another. By me. He's in a Romanian POW camp. Seriously wounded.

He's in a Romanian POW camp.

Seriously wounded.

He's in a Romanian POW camp.

Is he still there?

Or is he already gone?

They don't keep the seriously wounded for long.

No one needs seriously wounded soldiers . . .

*

The opposing sides in a conflict, as a rule, try to exchange the seriously wounded first. The seriously wounded are too much trouble. There is no time to save your own soldiers, let alone other peoples'. They're no fools. Expressing assurances of the utmost respect, the Red Cross attaches a new list of seriously wounded soldiers . . . Please, read it—they might die any day now . . .

Once, Lena, the typist, who lost her husband in early September, approached me and asked:

"Tanya, listen, you're one of them, right?"

"What do you mean?"

"You were born in the West, right?"

"Yes, in London."

"Listen, I keep typing all these documents and can't understand what's going on in their heads."

"In what sense?"

"I mean you Europeans. What's going on in your heads?"

"I'm a Soviet person and a Soviet citizen, just like you are."

"Oh, yes, of course, that's obvious! But since you've lived over there, you must understand what's going on in those people's heads."

"The same as in our heads, Lena."

"The same? No, I don't believe it! If it's the same, then why do they keep sending us all those documents?"

"What documents?"

"Well, all those letters where they talk about every single soldier. What do they do it for? What are they hoping to achieve? I don't understand this! Dozens of countries are fighting, hundreds of thousands are dying, but those clowns from Geneva send us letters. I wasted a lot of time today on three soldiers from the Kiev region. They all died, and there is no information about their relatives. What do they suggest I do?

Go to Ukraine and shout on the main square that I have three corpses?"

"Sometimes I think," she continued, "that those Swiss people just want to slow down our work. Maybe they're in with the fascists? Why do they care about what happens to us? What do they care if someone on our side dies? Why not send one combined list with the names at the end of the year? Do they really think that we don't have anything better to do than correspond with the relatives? When the war is over, everyone will figure it out!"

"I think they believe that it's important," I answered calmly, trying not to annoy Lena.

"What's important? Who cares about all this right now?"

"It's important to me. I'd like to know where my husband is right now."

"And what would that change?"

"Everything, Lena, everything . . ."

After throwing her cigarette butt on the ground, Tatyana went back to her office. Looking at the calendar, she realized she'd been smoking for a few weeks now. It calmed her down. Every day, she'd been waiting with horror for a death notification. Every night, she thought about the families she couldn't help. She tried to imagine the woman whom she'd placed under arrest twice and repeated the unknown soldier's name to herself, hoping he didn't have a family of his own. Tatyana was upset that she couldn't tell the thousands of mothers that their sons were alive and that she couldn't tell the others that their relatives were dead.

How could I have done that? Copy the list and send it out to everyone? But I wouldn't have had enough money for postage. Not to mention the fact that all letters from Moscow had to pass through the strictest censorship. Find those women and talk to them privately? But we worked without days off, and I couldn't

even leave the city. By then, I realized that I'd made a huge mis-
take. At the time, I felt like I'd found a good solution, but in
reality, it turned out to be the worst of all possible ones. How
could such a thought have entered my head? I could've filled in
any fictitious name, but instead, I made the most obvious
wrong move. What kind of idiot would you have to be to type
the same surname twice?! How could I have thought that the
NKVD wouldn't notice such an obvious coincidence? I
thought: As soon as they noticed the double entry, they'd real-
ize that something was fishy. Instead of writing a fake name
and diverting suspicion from my family, I did everything possi-
ble to prevent those bloodhounds not only from arresting a sol-
dier I didn't know but also from tracking me down.

There wasn't an hour in the day that she didn't think about
being arrested. Tatyana Alexeyevna was afraid for her husband; she was afraid for her daughter. Danger was waiting in
every corner at every moment. Tatyana waited for a knock on
her door. In anyone who so much as glanced at her, in every
passerby, she saw someone about to attack her. At night, after
putting Asya to bed, Tatyana Alexeyevna would listen to the
sound of the passing automobiles and fall asleep around three
or four o'clock in the morning, when her body was completely
exhausted.

She was designing an escape plan. Her only friend was in
prison. Lyosha's parents lived here, in Minsk, but by that time,
this was occupied territory, and that's why Tatyana Alexeyevna
was hesitating. Every time she'd come up with a plan, she'd
find obvious flaws in it. She had to act, but she was crippled by
fear.

"My maternal instinct wasn't helping me; it just forced me
to be more careful. I was scared. It seemed to me that all the
paths in this labyrinth led to prison. And it was terrifying.
Truly. That kind of pressure can drive you mad."

She felt like a prisoner who had been placed on death row but, for some reason, wasn't executed. A gun was pressed against the back of her head, its cold shaft was touching her neck, but the executioner would not pull the trigger. One day, two, twenty-two. After several months, she was so anxiety-ridden that she wanted to turn herself in.

I was constantly sick. My body was wearing out. Although it wasn't surprising in the least—as the harshest verdict is more humane that uncertainty.

From time to time, she had the same dream. Her husband took her by the hand, and they walked to a long wooden bridge. "Look," he said. "I built this bridge. But be careful—there was no time to put up railings." The bridge was built above a deep gorge and was shaking in the wind. Only with great caution could you walk, or better yet crawl, over the bridge. Every time they reached the middle, the husband and wife would stop for some reason and, instead of continuing their journey, they would go to the edge. Alexey would take Tatyana's hand and invite her to sit. She was scared to death but obeyed. Sitting with her legs dangling in the air while frozen with fear, Tatyana Alexeyevna would watch the tiny blue evergreen trees rustle down below. The bridge was swaying, and her hips became numb from fear. She would ask Alexey to let them continue crossing the bridge, but her husband wasn't there anymore. In the scariest moment of her life, he'd suddenly disappeared. She sat in the middle of that bridge and realized that if she even tried to get up, if she even tried to move back a bit, the bridge would sway, and she would fall . . .

+

I n April of 1942, the Red Cross sent one more document. This time the Romanians were proposing to repatriate 632 Soviet soldiers. Tatyana Alexeyevna made sure no one was watching, then checked the list again. Once, twice . . .

I read that document several times, but Lyosha's name wasn't there. There's no Lyosha . . . Is he feeling better? Did he recover? Did he run away? Have they transferred Lyosha to another camp? Is he already on his way back to Moscow?

She might have calmed herself down with the fact that her husband was alive. She might have even tried to convince herself that everything was going well for Alexey. She might have at least tried to tell herself, "Everything is okay with Alexey . . . Do you hear me? Do you hear me, you fool?! Look in the mirror and tell yourself, 'Everything is fine with Alexey!' Say it calmly and quietly . . . Breath out and say, 'Everything is fine with Alexey . . .'" But no, she couldn't do it. After several months of colossal pressure, Tatyana Alexeyevna gave up. She didn't have the strength. Lyosha's name wasn't on the new list, and Tatyana Alexeyevna was afraid that her husband was dead . . .

One day I saw my boss, Boris Podtserob, in the hallway, and I jumped up from my desk and ran after him:
"Boris Fyodorovich, we need to talk!"

"Why are you so upset, Tanya?"
"I need to ask you something—it's important!"
"I'm listening . . ."
"What will happen to our prisoners of war?"
"What do you mean, Tanya?"
"What will happen to our soldiers who were taken prisoner?"
"Why are you asking?"
"I'm afraid that my husband might be there . . ."

Suddenly more attentive, Podtserob asked her:
"Where, Tanya?"
"I'm not sure . . . It's just that there've been no letters from him for a long time, and I thought, what if he were taken prisoner?"
"Ah . . . but don't worry! You know how the mail works these days. Go back to work, everything'll be fine!"
"Boris Fyodorovich, my husband was on the Romanian list . . ."

It was a death sentence. She'd built the city and designed the square. She'd forged the blade and raised the executioner. She'd erected the scaffold and climbed to the top. All this lasted only a few seconds. Podtserob looked at Tatyana without saying a word, and she realized that she'd just convicted herself. After hearing her mention the Romanian list, Podtserob pushed her gently toward the window, looked around, and then asked quietly:
"Are you sure?"
"Yes."
"Is he on the last list of the seriously wounded?"
"No, he's not on the last one, but he was on the list that came in early winter. That's why I'm so nervous . . ."
"Forget about it!"
"What do you mean, Boris Fyodorovich?"

"Just forget it, do you hear me?"

"But how can I forget?"

"Just like that! He's not coming back! He'll never come back, understand?! Your husband will most likely die in the camp, and if he manages to run away and get back to our side, he'll immediately be arrested! Damn it, that's the last thing I need! There is no one to work as it is! Make sure no one finds out about this, do you hear?!"

"Yes, Boris Fyodorovich, but what will happen to him?"

"Nothing . . ."

Podtserob abruptly grabbed his papers from the windowsill and walked down the hallway. He was still whispering something to himself, and Tatyana realized that she'd committed a life-defining act of idiocy. She'd just executed herself. And Lyosha. And Asya.

Now my superior was required to write a report. If Podtserob kept my story quiet, he would basically be committing the crime of concealing a potential spy within the NKID. My boss disappeared behind a door, and I realized that there were only a few days before my arrest, which was now certain . . .

+

BRIEF
ON THE EXCHANGE OF INFORMATION RELATED
TO PRISONERS OF WAR

JANUARY 13, 1942. IN COMRADE VYSHINSKY'S REPORT ON THE EXCHANGE OF INFORMATION RELATED TO PRISONERS OF WAR FROM COUNTRIES FIGHTING AGAINST THE USSR, COMRADE MOLOTOV WROTE:

"THERE IS NO NEED TO SEND A LIST (THE GERMANS WILL BREAK ALL LEGAL AND OTHER NORMS)."

MARCH 24, 1942. COMRADE VYSHINSKY'S REPORT ON THE EXCHANGE OF THE PRISONER-OF-WAR LISTS WITH ROMANIA PROPOSED THAT WE NOT RESPOND TO THE RED CROSS'S OFFER TO EXCHANGE SUCH INFORMATION. THERE IS A NOTE INDICATING COMRADE MOLOTOV'S AGREEMENT WITH THAT POSITION.

APRIL 23, 1942. COMRADE VYSHINSKY'S REPORT ON THE NUMEROUS REQUESTS OF THE BULGARIAN MISSION REGARDING INFORMATION ABOUT GERMAN PRISONERS OF WAR IN THE USSR. MOLOTOV'S VERDICT:

"DO NOT RESPOND."

JULY 30, 1942. COMRADE VYSHINSKY'S REPORT REGARDING AN OFFER MADE BY THE FINNISH GOVERNMENT TO EXCHANGE PRISONER-OF-WAR LISTS. COMRADE MOLOTOV'S NOTE ON THE REPORT INDICATES HIS AGREEMENT THAT THIS OFFER BY THE FINNISH GOVERNMENT (ALONG WITH THE

CORRESPONDING TELEGRAM FROM THE INTERNATIONAL COMMITTEE OF THE RED CROSS) REQUIRES NO RESPONSE.

AUGUST 31, 1942. AT THE DIRECTION OF COMRADE VYSHINSKY, THE USSR AMBASSADOR IN SWEDEN WAS ADVISED NOT TO RESPOND TO THE REQUESTS OF THE SWEDISH MINISTRY OF FOREIGN AFFAIRS REGARDING THE EXCHANGE OF PRISONER-OF-WAR LISTS. IN THE EVENT THE SWEDES SHOULD INSIST, IT IS RECOMMENDED THAT THE PROPER AUTHORITIES BE TOLD THAT, DUE TO THE INHUMANE TREATMENT OF SOVIET PRISONERS OF WAR BY THE GERMANS AND THEIR ALLIES, THE NEGATIVE RESPONSE OF THE SOVIET GOVERNMENT IN REGARD TO THE EXCHANGE OF PRISONER-OF-WAR LISTS IS PERFECTLY UNDERSTANDABLE AND DOES NOT REQUIRE ANY EXPLANATION.

JANUARY 29, 1943. THE REPORT OF THE LEGAL DEPARTMENT TO COMRADE VYSHINSKY SUGGESTS THAT HE NOT RESPOND TO NOTE 27 FROM THE BULGARIAN MISSION DATED JANUARY 27, 1943 REGARDING THE INFORMATION REQUEST ON THE WHEREABOUTS OF THE GERMAN PRIVATE SECOND CLASS GASTANIEN WHO WAS CAPTURED BY THE RED ARMY. COMRADE VYSHINSKY'S VERDICT:

"AGREED."

+

In the middle of a field stood a cross. It was narrow and of human height. Simple but proud. Made from two old pipes, peeling and rust-covered, the cross appeared red. Leaning slightly, but lethally piercing the ground, this cross would vibrate with the first gust of wind and be transformed into a musical instrument. The cross sang about the past and the future, about death and desperation, about memory and humility. Not just wet but soaked in blood from below, from this very land, the cross was its history and metaphor, a warning and a landmark. Rains watered the cross, snow covered it, the sun burned it, and the shadow it cast was not black but a deep red. And now this shadow spread out so far across the horizon that, from time to time, people thought it was the sunset and stopped to admire it.

TELEGRAM
FROM GENEVA
25 JULY 1942
TO HIS EXCELLENCY MOLOTOV
THE PEOPLE'S COMMISSAR OF FOREIGN AFFAIRS
MOSCOW

THE FINNISH GOVERNMENT HAS ASKED US TO APPEAL AGAIN TO THE GOVERNMENT OF THE USSR WITH THE REQUEST TO OBTAIN INFORMATION ABOUT FINNISH PRISONERS OF WAR HELD BY THE SOVIET ARMY. THE LISTS THAT WE HAVE ALREADY RECEIVED FROM THE FINNISH GOVERNMENT CAN BE IMMEDIATELY EXCHANGED THROUGH OUR AGENCY AS SOON AS WE RECEIVE THE LISTS OF THE FINNISH PRISONERS OF WAR. IN THIS WAY, THE PRINCIPLE OF RECIPROCITY ACCEPTED IN ACCORDANCE WITH THE DECLARATIONS OF THE SOVIET AND FINNISH GOVERNMENTS IN 1941 CAN BE OBSERVED IN FULL AGREEMENT WITH THE HAGUE CONVENTION OF 1907 AND THE GENEVA CONVENTION OF 1929 REGARDING THE WOUNDED AND SICK.

CONSIDERING THE FACT THAT OUR MULTIPLE PROPOSALS TO SEND DELEGATIONS TO MOSCOW IN ORDER TO BEGIN THIS WORK HAVE GONE UNANSWERED, THE RED CROSS NOW SUGGESTS LIMITING OUR EFFORT TO THE MUTUAL AND SIMULTANEOUS MAILING OF INFORMATION ABOUT PRISONERS OF WAR

AND OFFERS TO PLAY THE ROLE OF MEDIATOR IN SUCH EXCHANGES.

ALONG WITH THIS TELEGRAM, THE INTERNATIONAL COMMITTEE OF THE RED CROSS IS SENDING YOUR EXCELLENCY A LETTER CONTAINING ADDITIONAL INFORMATION CONCERNING ALL ASPECTS OF THE QUESTION.

HUBER
INTERNATIONAL RED CROSS

"DO NOT RESPOND."

I bite my lip. My heart beats faster. I begin to understand that the story I'm about to hear is not going to be easy to listen to. In this moment, a stranger's bad luck mixes with mine. A reaction is taking place, and a detonator is being triggered. The bridge that I'd built so hastily collapses, and the memories of my wife return. A lump rises in my throat. I feel pressure in my chest. The sudden flush of emotions makes my stomach ache. I don't want to listen to all this—I've been through so much in the last few months.

"Sasha, is everything okay with you?"

"Yes, I think so, yes . . ."

"I wanted to ask why you moved here?"

"You already asked that."

"I forgot."

"As I told you, I thought it would be better for my daughter."

"Did you really say that? I don't remember. And what does your wife think about it? Moving is usually hard for women."

"And what difference does that make to you?" I suddenly lash out. "You wouldn't remember it anyway!"

"Tell me anyway."

"My wife doesn't live with us."

"How long has it been?"

"Already six months."

"What happened?"

"Listen, I don't think this is any of your business! I thought you wanted to tell me the story of fear, not to find out why I moved here. I didn't ask you to invite me over! What do you care about my story? Do you really need to stick your nose in your neighbors' business? And how are you settling in? And may I take a look? And why did you move? And what does your wife think about it?"

I get up. Pushing aside a painting that happens to be at my feet, I walk toward the front door. I pick up my groceries, jerk the door open and utter a rather rude "Have a good one!" My neighbor's lock clicks shut, and, a few seconds later, I'm finally in my own apartment. I walk straight into the kitchen, put the groceries away, and call my mom. The happy grandma tells me her granddaughter had a nice day. She was quiet, didn't fuss, and was happy to play with Grandpa. "I think she'll be a calm child," my mother concludes.

"That's great," I think.

I make a sandwich and open some vodka. There are no glasses, so I drink it straight from the bottle. My stomach is still bothering me, but with each gulp I feel the effects of that wonderfully numbing anesthetic.

Leaning against the wall, I think about my neighbor's story. What would I have done in her place? Would I have put my wife's name on the Russian list? I don't think so. This has nothing to do with my noble principles, but rather with my inability to come to a decision very fast. Even though I'm a soccer referee, quick decisions are not my strong suit. I'm shocked by her speed. Only the greatest soccer players can act like that on the field. Sometimes a single pass can determine the results of the entire game. Truth be told, people during Stalin's time had a phenomenal ability to estimate their own risk. I don't think I would ever have been able to cobble all the facts together so quickly. To realize in a second that my spouse's captivity could affect the future of our daughter . . . No, I wouldn't have been able to figure all that out in advance.

I raise the bottle of vodka and drink to the courage of one Soviet woman and also to the fact that, under similar circumstances, my life would've ended back in 1942 . . .

L ike every night lately, I dream about Lana. We're packing our suitcases. Judging by the swimming trunks and snorkeling masks, we're about to fly to the beach. I keep stepping over our stuff to kiss my wife. She's wearing a light summer dress. Even in my dream, I remember we bought it in Paris.

It was our first trip together. I was afraid my money would run out. We'd been dating for more than a year, but Lana still seemed to me to be from a different world. A beautiful woman who (for reasons I couldn't understand) still put up with me. Every time we stopped at a restaurant, I thought with horror that this was the moment I'd completely embarrass myself. I'd saved some money for one fancy dinner, which, naively, I expected to happen on the last day of our trip, as is the tradition.

The suitcase is packed. I'm beginning to close the zipper when someone rings the doorbell. This annoying visitor keeps ringing the bell, and I understand that if I don't close the suitcase right now, we'll be late for our vacation. I keep repeating, "Just a second, just a second," but the person at the door keeps ringing the bell until it finally wakes me up.

I open my eyes. It feels like I was asleep for only an hour, but the big hand of the clock is pointing to ten. Good morning, the movers have arrived. There are cabinets, chairs, and a sofa on the other side of the door.

"Just a second, guys, one second!"

The workers begin putting the furniture together, and I try to stay out of their way, taking my cup of coffee and going downstairs.

A light October rain is falling outside. The kindergarten kids watch the delivery truck being unloaded, peeking from behind the fence and holding onto the rails just like prisoners. I'm on the free side—they aren't. The boys, who seem to be from the older class, watch everything in attentive silence. With only slippers on my feet, I step over several puddles and walk up to the fence. One of the boys stretches his hand between the rails, greeting me like a grown-up:

"We ate Stalin today!"

"What did you do?" I ask, smiling.

"We ate Comrade Stalin!" the little boy answers with the same seriousness.

"What do you mean?"

"I ate the head but didn't like it—it was all dough!"

"And I ate his leg—it was made of chocolate!"

"And I ate his shoulder-boards and medals!"

"What do you mean, guys?"

"Today was Lyuda Kunitsyna's birthday, and her father brought us a cake in the shape of Comrade Stalin. He was surrounded by flowers and in a coffin, with chocolate."

"Was it really a life-size cake?"

"Yes!"

"No, not really!" the other boys chime in.

"Yes, it was!"

"No, it wasn't! Our teacher said that she was at the Mausoleum in Moscow and that the cake looks more like Lenin, because he was short."

"But did you like the cake?"

"Nah, Kiev cake with frosting mushrooms is better!"

I smile, throw away my cigarette, and finish my coffee, then tousle the little guy's hair. This is all we need to know about history: a tyrant who for decades kept his own citizens in a state of terror will inevitably rematerialize as a salad or a cake.

I started to feel a bit cold, so I decide to go back inside. Climbing the stairs, to my horror, I see my neighbor. "Damn her," I think.

"Good morning, Sasha!"

"Well, well! You're making progress."

"It's all because of the red crosses!"

"Listen, I want to apologize for yesterday. I overreacted . . ."

"Oh no, don't apologize! I understand. I shouldn't have asked you all those questions. You're right, I often meddle in other people's business. You know, after all these years I've become indifferent to human suffering—I see it as an intrinsic part of life, as something natural. Personally, I've never met happy people. I don't think such people exist. And unfortunately, it's very hard to shock me with misfortune. So, Sasha, will you forgive me?"

"Sure . . . but only if you forgive me."

I pass my neighbor and begin opening my door, but, once again, I hear her voice behind me:

"And still . . . you know . . . There was one detail that interested me. It could have been just a slip, but it's a very interesting one. You said yesterday that your wife left you six months ago, correct?"

"Yes, you could say that."

"But how old is your daughter?"

"She's three."

"Three months?"

"Damn it, yes."

"There! I don't know why, but I remembered that your daughter was only three months old. Even though I don't remember you telling me that."

"I did tell you that."

"You did? Hmm, okay . . . it must've slipped my mind. But you see, I remembered it this morning! I recalled it and thought, that all ends up being a rather strange story: the mom is gone for half a year, but the daughter is only three months old . . . How is that possible?"

"Old cow!" I think. "She just apologized for meddling but then goes and sticks her nose back where it shouldn't be. Does she really think I'll stay here in the middle of the staircase landing and tell her everything that happened to us?"

"Someday, by all means, I'll tell you everything, Tatyana Alexeyevna, someday . . . but only not today, okay? Excuse me, the movers are waiting for me."

+

In the evening of that same day, I go to my mom's. We sit in the living room. Mom plays with Liza while my stepfather is glued to the TV screen watching the Russian news.

"Ah, listen to them! Only fifteen years ago the whole world regarded us as equals, and now what? What do we fly? What will we fly? Pretty soon they'll have destroyed our entire air fleet! We'll be a second-rate people from a third-world country!"

"Speak for yourself!" mom says jokingly, keeping an eye on her granddaughter.

"Mom, I met my neighbor yesterday."

"The old lady?"

"Yeah."

"And what did you think of her?"

"She told me a lot of interesting things."

"That woman, the realtor, says that your neighbor spent many years in the Gulag."

"Really?"

"Yeah, in the Gulag. She probably stole something and got herself arrested!" my stepfather says, trying to be funny.

"Grisha, watch TV."

"Mom, what did the realtor tell you?"

"Nothing special. She said that she'd be a good neighbor, that she'd been in the Gulag, but that we shouldn't dwell on it, just buy the apartment—it's not easy to find decent neighbors these days."

"Decent neighbors! Anyone listening to you would think that everyone who'd been in the Gulag is decent! How do you know she's decent? Maybe she killed someone?"

"She worked in Moscow, at the MID . . ."

"And you think decent people work at the MID? They're all spies over there! They spend their whole lives whispering among themselves, and then they all make deals with the Americans, send their children over there to study, while they themselves . . ."

I keep quiet. I look at my mom and try to figure out why she moved to Minsk to be with this moron. My dad, of course, is no prize either, but this guy is a total idiot. What does my mom, a beautiful woman with a good sense of humor, see in this guy? Meanwhile, my stepfather is not calming down.

"They've looted everything! Everything! It's good we have a real leader—he'll get things back in order pretty quickly! If only we could send another Stalin to Russia! He'd put everybody in front of a firing squad, and everything would be fixed!"

"They ate your Stalin."

"What?"

"They ate your Stalin, just like I said. And he didn't even taste that good."

"Sasha, what are you talking about?"

"Oh, it's nothing. Uncle Grisha, listen. I wanted to ask you if pilots drink when they're flying?

"Of course they drink!"

"But how? Don't they check you before the flight?"

"Yes, they do, before the flights, but not during or after! The flight attendants serve us drinks. How do you think I met your mom?"

"I see. Mom, listen, I probably won't stay over tonight. I need to get used to my new place."

"That's okay, dear. By the way, have you decided anything about work?"

"Yeah, some people have promised to help."

I kiss my mom and daughter and go outside. At night, Minsk doesn't look so scary. I like that it's so calm here. The cars hide, and so do the people. Walking back home, I listen to Liszt's *Hungarian Rhapsody* on my CD player. Recalling everything my neighbor told me, it seems that the value of a human life will never increase. It's the cheapest commodity there is. The arrangement may change, but the motif stays the same. Blood will flow as it always has because that's human nature. Blood will flow forever because if blood suddenly stops flowing in a human body, that person will die, as my friend Pasha says.

In the metro, I look at the people and the ads. A bright poster urges me to buy a game console and the soccer simulator that goes with it. "That game was poorly developed," I think. "It's strange that the developers still haven't come up with a mode where you can be the referee. They now have settings where you can play by yourself or with a few friends. You can even crack open a beer and watch how AI plays with itself, but there's no referee mode. Don't the developers of sports games realize that being a referee is the most exciting role and at the same time the hardest one?"

Nothing has changed. I come back home, and once again I see my neighbor on the landing. After shaking the raindrops off my jacket, I realize she doesn't recognize me.

"Have you been standing here all day?"

"Who are you?"

"My name is Alexander. I'm your new neighbor."

"Really? Nice to meet you! I'm Tatyana Alexeyevna. I'm the one who drew a red cross on your door. I have Alzheimer's. So far, it's only my short-term memory that's affected, but very soon I'll start forgetting everything that's happened to me during my life."

"I'm very sorry!" I repeat yet again for some reason.

"Don't worry! That's the only way things could have ended up for me," my neighbor says, pausing. But this time I don't ask, "Why?"

"So, you're going to live here now?"

"Yes."

"By yourself?"

"With my daughter."

"What do you do for a living?"

"I'm a soccer referee."

"Oh, wow! That must be an interesting job! My husband loved soccer. He even had the chance to root for Spartak for a while. Is it difficult?"

"To root for Spartak?"

"No, no, I mean to be a referee. Is it difficult to be a judge?"

"Yeah, at times it's not easy."

"All the pressure, right?"

"There's that too," I answer with a sigh while leaning against the railing.

"How do they teach you to handle it?"

"Are you really interested?"

"Of course! Or why would I be asking?"

"So, how do they teach us . . . When you decide to become a referee, they give you a little book with the rules and talk to you about responsibility. They explain to you that you affect the outcome of the game without participating in it. In general, they tell you pretty obvious things until one fine day they deliver a simple truth, "If you screw up, do it with confidence!"

"Yes, that's a good rule. It's a pity that it's followed mostly by our leaders, not by our judges."

"It's hard to disagree with you on that. Oh, well, it's already late. Sleep well, Tatyana Alexeyevna!"

"All the best to you too, Sasha!"

"By the way, I bought some groceries. There's milk, bread, sugar . . . if you need anything . . ."

"Thanks, but I don't eat sugar—I'm watching my figure."

"What about the other things?"

"The other things, Alexander, I can buy myself. I'm only ninety-one."

"Ninety-one and without a clue where the store is."

"There's no need to be rude, young man!"

"Okay, okay . . . I won't be! But really, if you need anything, please, ask. I'm always happy to help you."

"Truly?"

"Yes."

"Then I do have a favor I want to ask you. You won't say no, will you?"

"Damn . . ." I think to myself.

"Would you stop by for a minute?"

"Yes, of course!"

When I'm in her apartment again, I decide not to repeat my mistakes from yesterday. Tatyana Alexeyevna goes into the living room, but I stay in the entry hall. A few minutes later she comes back holding a piece of paper.

"What's that?"

"An epitaph. I wanted to ask you to have these words put on my tombstone. I don't know who'll bury me. I used to think it would be Yadviga, but she's been very sick lately."

I open the piece of paper, read the five words written on it, then smile and promise to fulfill her request.

"Does that mean I can count on you?"

"Yes, don't worry."

"Who are you going to live with here?"

"No one."

"No one? What about your wife? You're so handsome—for some reason I thought for sure you'd have a wife."

"Damn it! Tatyana Alexeyevna, please, don't start!"

"What did I say that's so wrong? Do you have a wife or not?"

"Yes . . . I used to . . ."

"She just came and went, is that it?"

"Damn it, yes!"

"Why are you so irritated, Sasha? It's all damn this and damn that with you. How did you meet?"

"What's the difference?"

"There's a difference, my dear, a big difference! When two people meet, it's always a beautiful thing. The sorrows come later."

"We met just like everybody else."

"And how's that, 'like everybody else?'"

"At a party, at a fairly ordinary party."

"Here, in Minsk?"

"No, in Yekaterinburg."

"So, tell me about it!"

"But I don't want to."

"But I'm asking you to!"

"Tatyana Alexeyevna, I'm telling you that we met the way everyone meets! Can I go now?"

"An old woman's asking you a question, is that so difficult? Tell me first, and then you're free to go wherever you like!"

I lean against the door, let out a deep sigh, put the bag of groceries on the floor, and say:

"Actually, I wasn't planning to go to that party, but my friend insisted, saying there'd be some cool girls."

"And she was the coolest, is that right?"

"Yes, she was. Actually, it wasn't an ordinary party—there

were some local celebrities: the guy who sang about Argentina's victory over Jamaica; the poet who wrote, 'Before you get in a tractor crash, shoot yourself, or drown in a river.' The musician, whose work I'd never liked, turned out to be a surprisingly nice guy, while the talented poet was the opposite, a total bore. I liked his poetry a lot, but he acted weird."

"That's normal for a poet."

"His behavior was normal for a punk, but that's okay. To be honest, I felt pretty weird myself. You know, all those conversations in provincial high society . . . it's quite a cocktail—I'd even say a Molotov cocktail. So, I stood around for a while and was going to leave when she suddenly approached me.

'Are you leaving?'

'Yes, I have practice tomorrow,' I said.

'Are you an athlete?'

'Not quite. I'm a referee.'

'Really? Then you must know how important it is to follow the rules.'

'And?'

'And to not leave the field before the game's over.'

'I shouldn't even be here. My friend dragged me here at the last minute.'

'Does that mean I'll owe my future marriage to your friend?'"

"Wow, I thought. What a woman! She's known me for less than a minute, and she's already flirting.

'I don't think we've met,' I noted, shyly.

'I'd known my first husband since first grade, but it didn't save our marriage. It'd be a pity to make the same mistake again.'

'That's why you've decided to marry me?'

'Yes, and why not? You're modest, good-looking, and it seems you're often away from home.'

'Are you planning to cheat on me?'
'No, never. That was a bad joke.'
'Should we leave?'
'I was afraid you'd never ask.'"

So that's how we met. An ordinary walk. He's shy, she's bold. I tried to joke, and Lana, it seems, even laughed. It was a good evening. It lasted several hours, but in a movie, it would've been shot as one long frame. With upbeat music, filled with basses and percussion. I was walking ahead, explaining soccer to her, and she was smiling. Narrow streets, hand in hand, my jacket hung on a finger over my shoulder. The next night, Lana moved in with me.

"Is Lana short for Svetlana?"

"No, it's an Old Slavic name."

"What does it mean?"

"Earth."

"And was Lana beautiful?"

"Very! After our first night together, I was on my way to a game, and I thought of her as being like a final wish. If I were condemned to death and given a last wish, I'd ask to look at her one more time. I closed my eyes and smiled, understanding that from now on I'd be fearless, that nothing would scare me anymore, and that there was no death because there was Lana. I couldn't believe my luck. When Lana kissed me for the first time, I thought there was some mistake. Offside by a meter. Eighty thousand people in the stadium saw that I was offside, but for some reason, the referee didn't raise a flag. Damn, Tatyana Alexeyevna, it was all so good . . ."

"And what came afterward?"

"Happiness. We were perfectly matched. We would talk and never be disappointed. We would talk and agree with each other, we would smile, and we were happy. Lana got pregnant in November of 2000, during our Paris trip. Could there be anything more beautiful than that and more clichéd?"

"And?"

"And what?"

"You said that your wife left."

"*You* said that."

"Okay, I'll ask you one more time: What happened with your wife?"

I stop talking and look down. At my dirty shoes. How stupid! It was stupid to buy suede shoes for fall. I've been wearing them for less than a week, but they look like they're several years old. Plus, they're cold . . . I thought the fall was warmer in Minsk. "I'll wear them with warm socks," I think.

"Alexander!"

"Yes?"

"I asked what happened with your wife?"

"I told you she got pregnant."

"And is that the end of the story?"

"More like the first half. Along with the wonderful news came the first bouts of pain. Tests showed that Lana had cancer. I remember sitting in my friend's office, the same friend who'd invited me to that party. We were examining the X-rays and listening to him—as he calmly explained to us that the situation was hopeless. Like love. I now realize that, on that day, I was less shocked by the diagnosis than by his calm demeanor as he explained it to us.

'And how long do I have left?' Lana asked.

'It's hard to say. We know of many surprising cases, but I wouldn't plan on more than three months.'

'Three months?'

'Yes . . . well, four months, maximum. The tumor is inoperable. There's nothing we can do. In layman's terms, the tumor cells will eat your brain. The only thing I can recommend now is that you make sure you have good pain relief. Fortunately, there's no problem getting painkillers here in Yekaterinburg.'

'Yes, we'll find them. So, your prognosis is five to six months?'

'I said three to four.'

'Yes, darling, he said three to four.'

'How far along are you, Lana?'

'A couple of weeks.'

'We'll have an abortion.'

'No!'

'What do you mean, no?'

'I don't want to have an abortion.'

'Listen, it's not a choice. I could've approached this discussion differently. I could have turned everything inside out, like a glove, beginning with the fact that you should have an abortion because the pregnancy could aggravate your condition and even lead to death. But then you would've guessed that the diagnosis was bad. And I don't believe that's the right way to talk to a patient, especially to a close friend. Unfortunately, in your case, that moment is past. Or to be precise, that moment was never there.'"

I remember how we sat on a bench in front of the hospital. I held Lana's hand and tried to understand why this misfortune had dropped on us out of the blue. I felt pressure in my chest, and a lump rose in my throat. I was moving my tongue inside my cheek so as not to burst into tears.

"I think we should try," Lana said calmly.

"Of course! I'm sure it'll work for us."

"No, my darling, I'm not talking about that. That's all pretty clear . . . I'm talking about something else: I think I'll have enough time to give birth."

"Yes, but . . ."

"But what?"

"Chemotherapy and all the drugs you'll be taking . . . They try to keep pregnant women as drug-free as possible, but you'll be under a chemical assault."

"Well, I won't take anything. I'll live as long as God allows."

"Why don't we try to beat the disease first, and then we'll try again for a baby?"

"Because we can't beat it. A hundred years from now, people will laugh at us; they'll probably feel sorry for us. I'm sure that someday cancer will be easily treatable, but you see, it's not today, not now. Please, let's not talk about it. You heard what Maxim said. There won't be a second chance, there won't be a fight. You can't run a hundred meters in seven seconds, and I can't cheat death. At least give me a chance to become a mother! I've been dreaming about it all my life! Please, don't leave me . . ."

Lana squeezed my hand, and I fell silent. In my life, I'd only studied at the university and taken some classes on how to be a referee. I'd never studied situations like this. It was a problem without any correct solutions. I kept peeling paint off the bench with my index finger, and gulping. Lana was rubbing her stomach while I looked down at the cracks in the pavement.

We went to the marriage registration office the very next morning. We submitted our marriage application and then went back to see the doctor. Lana explained to him that, despite everything, she wanted to keep the baby. Max tried to stay calm:

"It's your choice, but I'll explain to you again—you don't have enough time. Instead of one death, there'll be two. It's very sad for me to talk about it, but everything will be over much sooner than you might expect."

"Everything is always over much sooner then we might expect."

Lana was not backing down. She said it was her final decision.

"If you don't help us, I'll find another doctor!"

"I would gladly refer you to someone else, but it wouldn't be of any use in this case."

"Maybe I should go somewhere? To England, or to Switzerland?"

"No . . . I don't think that makes any sense."

"But I'm sure they can extend my life for just half a year?"

"No, no one can."

"So, what do you suggest? That I just lie down and die? I'm not asking for myself!"

"I suggest you have an abortion now, and then we'll do everything possible to ease your pain."

"What kind of pain? Physical?"

Lana wouldn't agree to it. We got married one month later. It was a very modest ceremony. Without a white dress and guests. "She probably got knocked up," thought the experienced clerk at the marriage registration bureau. True, that's how it was. We sold my car and used the money for the necessary drugs. I need to mention here that Maxim helped us a lot. I'm sure you know that doctors don't like to waste their time on terminal patients. When they decide to take on such a patient, it's only if it's an interesting case. Lana's wasn't. Her fate was already clear. Moreover, the disease was progressing faster than planned. There was a high degree of predictability. The winning coefficient was one in a billon. Nevertheless, my friend was able to convince his colleagues that Lana deserved a dignified death.

"Believe me, she's a very good person."

Good people deserve a peaceful death. That's how we got a single room. A tiny one, but it was ours. With Max's permission, I fixed up the room, hung blinds on the windows, and brought books from home. Lana was a good sport. Every time I entered the room, she would be in good spirits. She didn't complain and didn't whine. Of course, we often discussed serious issues, but even in such moments Lana found the strength to joke.

"You know, I read today that Solzhenitsyn said cancer loves people—if it falls in love with someone, it'll never leave.' It means that it's in love with me. It means that I'm going to give you a daughter, but at the same time I'm cheating on you. But you'll forgive me, darling, won't you?"

"Very funny!"

Now I realize that I was often unable to find the right words. At night, when my wife was drifting off to sleep, I would go to a bar or to a party. It was always the same poet, Boris Ryzhy, reciting the same poem:

Don't leave me when things are good,
When stars are shining bright,
When everything and everywhere
Seems so perfect, seems so right.

Don't leave me for a reason,
But just like that and, by the way,
Leave me when I'm feeling pain,
Leave me then and go away.

Let the heavens empty out,
Let the forests turn to ash,
Let the terror come at night,
Before I close my eyes.

Death's angel, she enters late,
Slipping poison in the wine,
Reshuffling all the cards of fate,
Then lays a joker down.

Stay right there, off to the side,
Whiter than a white cherry tree,
And, without touching, laugh,
While stretching out a hand to me.

The guests applaud languidly, and I ask Max how I should talk with my wife. My friend tries to calm me down by explaining that even doctors don't know what to say in such situations.

"You can simply nod and say nothing. It's not that difficult."

When I entered the hospital room the next morning, I saw my wife sitting on the windowsill. Lana was rubbing her belly and telling our daughter:

"Don't worry, sweetheart, your daddy will take care of you . . . Ah, here he is! Look how handsome your daddy is!"

Lana was whispering, "Daddy will take care of you," and there was so much serenity and assurance in her words that even I felt their calming effect. I wiped away my tears and went up to my wife.

"Oh, you're such a fool! You can cry here! If they didn't teach boys from a very early age to hold back their tears, this world would be a much better place, kinder and more balanced. By the way, while we're talking about this world, we need to decide where we'll meet—I need to know where to wait for you."

"Well . . . maybe up there, in heaven, it's hard to miss each other."

"No-no-no! You can't do things like that! Don't you understand, it has to be a specific place!"

"But you know I'm not great at picking places."

"Maybe Mars? What do you think?"

"Yeah, that's not a bad idea. Why not?"

"And we also need to think about a name. Do you want us to pick it together, or would you rather do it later?"

"I think I want you to choose the name."

"Maybe Nadya? What if she were called Nadezhda?"

"Are you kidding? *Hope*? Lana, quit it!"

"Okay, okay! Where's your sense of humor? Is your wife dying or something?"

"Screw you, Lana!"

"I'm already screwed. So, what about the name?"

"Maybe we could call her Lana?"

"Like me? No! No way! A new person is coming into the world, not the continuation of an old one. Promise me you'll be strong, that you'll be able to live with this from the very first days."

"I promise."

"That's a good boy! But now, please, leave. I need to be alone for a while."

"Already?"

"Yes."

Whenever the pain started, I would go find a nurse and then wouldn't return to the room for several hours. Lana didn't want me to see her like that.

We spent all winter in the hospital room. During the spring I refereed a lot of games. Because of the weather, most of them were held indoors. Amateur, adult, and youth competitions. The extra money was a very welcome thing. During one of those games, at halftime, Maxim called and told me that Lana had died. It was the fifth month. My friend said he was sorry and explained that everything had gone smoothly.

"Can I finish the game?"

"Yes, everything's in order. You can finish giving away your red cards and come here after the game."

A red card. Dismissal.

I remember on that day I was refereeing an amateur tournament organized by a local radio station. A team of police officers was playing a team of seminary students. The law enforcement team felt complete impunity, as was typical of that time, and so they were constantly rude and used their elbows. At first, the seminarians tolerated it, but in the second half, they began misbehaving in return. At one moment, I was lost in thought and missed a crucial foul. As a result, a fight erupted on the field.

A soccer player always has the right to make a mistake. He can make a bad pass, miss the goal, or turn the ball over to the other team. A referee doesn't have that right. When you're a referee, you've got to understand that you're always in the center of conflicts. The moment you step on the field, you have twenty-two opponents, and you play against them. And it all comes down to who will overpower whom. You have to make them play by your rules, or they'll destroy you. The players are like the masses—when they smell the tiniest drop of blood, that's it, you're done for.

The most important thing for a referee is choosing the form of punishment. Unfortunately, understanding the degree of punishment allowable only comes with time. The players have to know what you'll definitely punish them for and what you'll let slide. I call it your perception of justice. Yes, exactly like with dictators or gods. The players are extremely sensitive to each of your decisions. They think you're not judging them fairly. It's important to find a reasonable man on each team so that you can explain to the other players, through him, what's happening on the field. A game is a living process, and it's more important to apply the law evenly than to always apply it correctly. If a referee follows the rules to the letter, believe me, he'll very quickly lose control of the game. Well, that's exactly what happened on that day. Thinking about my wife's death, I didn't really pay attention to the game, and so I applied the rules mechanically. But when the fight broke out, I simply stopped the game, gave out the cards, and went to the showers after writing my report.

On the surface, nothing had changed. It was as if Lana hadn't died. The monitors continued working, and I saw that my wife had a pulse, just like before. A human being had died, but her heart was still beating . . .

Max went with me to the hospital room and stood behind me for some time, and then he took my hand and led me out. We sat across from each other. It was so quiet in the hallway that I could hear the heartbeat of my recently deceased wife. Max wiped his eyes with his right hand, as if it were a handker-chief, and began talking calmly:

"Well, now everything is happening as we've discussed over the past few weeks. Lana has passed away. In fact, she's dead. Her brain is dead, it's stopped working, and that's the end. As a person, Lana no longer exists, and so you mustn't be confused by what's happening. We can never have her back, and the only difference is that her funeral won't be tomorrow, but several months from now. Do you understand this?"

"Yes," I said quietly.

"Good, so that's clear. Now let's talk about the baby. She's in good shape. We weren't completely sure before, but Lana's heart continued working, so we decided to take the risk. We'll try to save the girl. Everything will happen exactly as I explained to you. For several months, we'll support life in her body, we'll help her heart and kidneys function properly, we'll monitor all the vital processes in Lana's body. Again, we'll arti-ficially support all her bodily functions—we'll use a respiratory machine and powerful circulatory drugs. Nurses will monitor the fetus twenty-four hours a day, and when the baby is ready, we'll deliver her by C-section."

"That means in two or three months?"

"Yes, as soon as it's feasible."

"But how will the baby feel? Does she understand that her mom has died?"

"It's difficult to answer that question. We've never done anything like this before."

"But Lana's body won't decay?"

"No," Maxim said with a barely noticeable smile. Of course, he wasn't smiling about the situation, only about my ignorant question. "I've already explained it to you a hundred times! Only her brain has died. All her bodily processes will be supported artificially, and Lana, if I may use the comparison, will look like she's asleep. I think it will be very helpful if you keep stopping in here."

"Wait, Sasha, I don't completely understand. You mean your wife died, but the doctors decided to save the baby?"

"Yes. Maxim thought Lana would die in late May or early June. When in July, Lana was still alive despite everything, it became clear that it was possible to save the baby. Max came to the hospital room a few weeks before Lana's death and said that, considering the stage of the pregnancy, he wanted to propose something. He wasn't promising anything, but he believed we could try. As he explained, the cancer cells affected only the brain and, therefore, there was a high probability the rest of the organs should be capable of functioning even after death."

"And Lana agreed?"

"Yes, she was happy. Actually, we couldn't have dreamed of anything more. It became clear with time that Lana wouldn't last until her seventh month, and that we'd have to rely on doctors."

"My God . . ."

"That night when I came home, I turned on the TV and watched documentaries about space exploration on the Discovery channel. A famous actor was talking about new expeditions to Mars. It was fascinating. And it was a good distraction. The next morning, I went back to the hospital, sat next to my wife, and, accompanied by the noise of the monitors, I told my daughter that traveling to Mars was a real possibility. I told her that a Martian day lasts for 24 hours, 37 minutes, and 35.244 seconds, which is very close to a day on Earth. The monitors continued to beep as I told her that the seasons change on Mars, just like on Earth, and that the temperature at Mars's equator was sometimes +20°C. Mars, I went on, has an atmosphere and water. So, life is possible, guys, life is possible.

"In the hospital's courtyard, I would look up at the sky, see a passing plane, and imagine that one day, maybe twenty years from now, my daughter would go to Mars. I imagined that a quarter of a century from now, when even the most intractable problems would be solved, when pharmacologists would make their money off something new, when cancer, having exhausted its financial potential, would be treated like a runny nose, our daughter would lead the first expedition to the red planet and she'd find her mom there. Why? Because several weeks before we'd agreed on that."

"It must have been a tough time."

"It wasn't easy. It was more like a dream. When rumors about Lana's death started to circulate, it got even harder. Almost every day, I had to discuss what was going on with someone new. Her friends and relatives were coming to the hospital. Everyone wanted to pay their respects to Lana but, to my great relief, Maxim ordered all visitors to remain in the waiting room. Journalists tried to visit, and so did idle gawkers who pretended to be old friends of Lana. Even her ex showed up. He put a few carnations on a chair and hugged me as if we'd been friends all our lives. Some actor! Lana had left that man, but suddenly he starts inundating me with his problems, saying that he'd never loved anyone as much as he'd loved Lana. In the end, that idiot sputtered something to the effect that this baby was in some way his too.

"My father came the next day. For several minutes, he talked about something irrelevant and then asked the only question that mattered to him:

'What are you going to do?'

'What do you mean, Dad?'

'You need to think about all of this very carefully, son . . .'

'And what exactly do I need to think about?'

'As I said, about everything . . .'

'Are you saying you don't want to become a grandfather?'

'Well, maybe I do, but the whole situation is rather strange. People are saying things . . .'

'And what are people saying?'

'That all this is no good.'

'And what's no good about it?'

'Well, it's not how people are supposed to do these things. It's all very strange.'

'Is it strange to save a life?'

'No, that's not it. Don't interrupt me. Listen to me. Lana has died. The Lord has taken her. That means He's called her along with her little girl, but you and the doctors are fighting against His will.'

'Father, do you even realize what you're saying?'

'What am I saying? Sasha, let's be honest. I understand that for you, for all of us, this is an enormous tragedy. But you can't let it go on like this! We all know that in less than two hours after death irreversible processes take place in the human body.'

'And when did you become a medical doctor?'

'Well, maybe I'm no doctor, but I understand that what

you're doing here is nonsense. Think about it: how is this child supposed to live? First, without a mother, second, when they learn her story in school—you realize she'll be bullied, right?'

'There won't be any bullying! I've already decided that we'll move away from here.'

'Where would you move?'

'Any place, it doesn't matter.'

'Well, I don't know. It's your decision, of course, but think about it some more. Maybe it'd be better to bury Lana?'

'Do you suggest that I bury that child alive?'

'How can you bury someone who hasn't been born yet?'

'Dad, the girl is there, inside, and she's alive.'

'But if you take Lana off life support, the baby will die too.'

'So now you're suggesting that we kill her?'

'I suggest following the natural course of things, as people do. Think about it: even now, as you and I are arguing, she's not buried. How can her soul find peace while we're doing this to her? Don't you understand that you've made your wife a prisoner of your own sorrow?'

'I understand that you're a prisoner of your own ignorance, father.'

'You're already angry? And I came to talk about this calmly. I understand that the first year will be very hard for you, but nothing can be done here—this is your cross.'

'Thanks for stopping by, Dad.'

"The priest came right after my dad left. I didn't expect anything good from his visit but, fortunately, I was wrong. The priest was kind and calm. He came to support me and, surprisingly, he was very sympathetic:

'Now people will tell you many things, Alexander, they'll probably even use quotations from the Bible to support their silliness, but you shouldn't pay any attention to them. You should pray, Alexander, you should pray! You pray, and I will pray for you! I want you to know that you are not doing anything wrong; on the contrary, you're saving a new life—and this is the only thing of importance, and there is nothing more important than that!'

'Thank you, Father . . .'

'Father Sergiy.'

'Thanks, Father Sergiy! It's only a pity that I don't believe in your boss.'

'I understand. That's all right. I'll be praying for you! Most importantly, don't give up!'

"The surgery went well. Liza was born weighing a little over a kilogram, and she was instantly taken to the intensive care unit. 'Now we're waiting again,' Max said, patting me on the shoulder. 'But congratulations! You're a father!'

"For thirty days my daughter was connected to machines, then she spent another month in the hospital. During that time, I began preparations for our move to Minsk, and I buried my wife. I know it sounds strange, but I liked the funeral. It was a calm and dignified ceremony. No one was screaming, no one was crying. I can't remember all the details now, but I think Father Sergiy said a few simple, straightforward words."

"Sasha . . ." Tatyana Alexeyevna whispers, "forgive me! I'm an old fool! You're right, I'm always sticking my nose in other people's business."

"It's okay. It's nothing."

We're sitting in the vestibule. We're quiet. Just me and my neighbor. The light flickers in a solitary bulb. We remain quiet for some time, then out of blue, Tatyana Alexeyevna says:

"You're a strong man, Sasha. It's difficult for me even to imagine what you had to go through."

"Nonsense."

"Yes, believe me! I've seen a lot! I understand what you're feeling now."

"Well, maybe you're right. I don't know. Listen, I wanted to ask you something."

"Yes?"

"I wanted to ask how you ended up in the Gulag."

"How do you know that I ended up in the Gulag?"

"You told me."

"Really? I don't remember that at all."

"Did it happen in 1942, when the lists arrived?"

"Did I tell you about the lists too?"

"Yes."

"No, they didn't touch me in 1942. I got lucky in 1942. Nothing happened. *Live as you used to live. Go to work, Tanya, go to work. Why are you standing around?!*"

Tatyana Alexeyevna continued working at the NKID. After meeting with an envoy, Solomon Lozovsky, the secretary to the Deputy Commissar—whose handwriting she hated—would throw the transcript of another conversation on her desk. She would try to hide her nervousness and type yet another of the thousands of internal documents:

MEETING
WITH SWEDISH AMBASSADOR ASSARSSON
6 JULY 1942

ASSARSSON WAS SOMEWHAT HESITANT AND DISINCLINED TO DISCUSS THIS TOPIC. HE SAID THAT HE DID NOT TRUST THE FASCISTS, BUT THAT HE WANTED TO TALK TO ME ABOUT ANOTHER, MORE GENERAL ISSUE. THE POPE HAD REQUESTED THAT THE SWEDISH GOVERNMENT APPROACH THE SOVIET GOVERNMENT WITH A PROPOSITION TO ORGANIZE, THROUGH

THE MEDIATION OF THE VATICAN, A CAMPAIGN TO INFORM THE OFFICIALS INVOLVED ABOUT THE CONDITIONS OF SOVIET PRISONERS OF WAR IN GERMANY AND ABOUT THE CONDITIONS OF GERMAN AND ITALIAN PRISONERS OF WAR IN THE USSR. THE POPE BELIEVES THAT HE WILL RECEIVE A POSITIVE RESPONSE FROM THE GERMAN GOVERNMENT AND HOPES FOR A POSITIVE RESPONSE FROM THE SOVIET GOVERNMENT. ASSARSSON ADDED THAT THE EMBASSY WOULD GLADLY UNDERTAKE THE MEDIATION AS HE BELIEVES AN AGREEMENT ON THIS PROPOSAL WOULD MAKE A VERY GOOD IMPRESSION AS THIS IS A MATTER OF HUMANITY AND UNIVERSAL HUMAN VALUES.

I ANSWERED ASSASSON THAT I WOULD PASS ON HIS INQUIRY TO MY GOVERNMENT BUT THAT, IN MY PERSONAL OPINION, THE PROPOSAL WAS UNACCEPTABLE. IN THIS PARTICULAR CASE, WE ARE NOT DEALING WITH A REGULAR GOVERNMENT, BUT WITH BANDITS AND KILLERS, WHO BRUTALIZE, TORTURE, AND KILL PRISONERS OF WAR, OLD PEOPLE, WOMEN, AND CHILDREN. THESE KILLERS BREAK ALL NORMS OF INTERNATIONAL LAW, ALTHOUGH THEY DO NOT MIND USING INTERNATIONAL LAW TO SERVE THEIR OWN INTERESTS. I DOUBT THAT THE SOVIET GOVERNMENT WILL AGREE TO THIS PROPOSAL. IT IS IMPOSSIBLE TO DEAL WITH THESE GANGSTERS, EVEN WITH THE MEDIATION OF THE VATICAN.

ASSARSSON UNDERTOOK TO PERSUADE ME THAT IT WAS IN OUR BEST INTEREST TO ACCEPT THE HOLY FATHER'S OFFER BECAUSE, REGARDLESS OF THE FASCISTS' INTENTIONS, IT WOULD GIVE US AN OPPORTUNITY TO OBTAIN INFORMATION AND PASS IT ON TO RUSSIAN FAMILIES THAT WANT TO KNOW ABOUT THE CONDITION OF THEIR RELATIVES.

I ANSWERED THAT, WHILE THE SUFFERING OF SOVIET PEOPLE IS VERY CLOSE TO OUR HEARTS, WE SHOULD NOT DEAL WITH THE KILLERS WHO NOW RULE GERMANY BECAUSE THEY MIGHT PROVIDE INFORMATION THAT A PERSON IS ALIVE

WHILE KNOWING FOR A FACT THAT THE GESTAPO HAD KILLED THAT PERSON MANY MONTHS AGO.

ASSARSSON BEGAN ARGUING THAT THIS WAS NOT A BIG ISSUE AND THAT OUR AGREEMENT TO PARTICIPATE IN THIS INITIATIVE WOULD BENEFIT ALL MANKIND.

I ANSWERED HIM THAT THIS WAS NOT A MINOR ISSUE, BUT THAT IT WAS MORE A MATTER OF PRINCIPLE. WHEN HITLER'S GOVERNMENT KILLS HUNDREDS OF THOUSANDS OF PRISONERS OF WAR AND EXTERMINATES THE CIVILIAN POPULATION, WE SHOULD NOT ENTER INTO RELATIONS WITH SUCH A GOVERNMENT. AGAIN, I STRESSED THAT THIS WAS ONLY MY PERSONAL OPINION AND PROMISED TO PASS ON THE PROPOSAL OF THE SWEDISH GOVERNMENT TO MY GOVERNMENT.

ASSARSSON SAID GOODBYE AND NOTED THAT HE WAS LEAVING MY OFFICE DISAPPOINTED. WITH THAT THE MEETING WAS OVER.

There was no time to be bored. There were mysteries to be mass produced, secrets to be manufactured. Lozovsky's assistant showed up again and again, providing Tatyana Alexeyevna with the next list and giving her only ten minutes to complete everything. She would rub her eyes and continue working. Day after day she typed out the documents, took all the information in, and tried to imagine her husband's situation.

USSR
FROM THE PEOPLE'S COMMISSARIAT OF FOREIGN AFFAIRS
TO THE HEAD OF THE CENTRAL BUREAU OF PERSONAL
RECORDS OF MILITARY PERSONNEL LOST IN COMBAT

I AM FORWARDING YOU THE GERMAN, ROMANIAN, AND ITALIAN LISTS OF SOVIET PRISONERS OF WAR AND THE LISTS OF DECEASED SOVIET PRISONERS OF WAR RECEIVED BY THE

NKID THROUGH THE INTERNATIONAL COMMITTEE OF THE RED CROSS.

I WOULD LIKE TO DRAW YOUR ATTENTION TO THE FACT THAT WE DO NOT RESPOND TO THE NUMEROUS PROPOSALS FROM THE RED CROSS CONCERNING THE EXCHANGE OF INFORMATION ABOUT PRISONERS OF WAR WITH THE GERMANS AND THEIR ALLIES. WHEN USING THE ABOVE-MENTIONED LISTS, YOU SHOULD TAKE THIS CIRCUMSTANCE INTO CONSIDERATION AND REFRAIN FROM INITIATING ANY CORRESPONDENCE WITH THE INTERNATIONAL COMMITTEE OF THE RED CROSS ON THIS SUBJECT.

AT THE SAME TIME, I WOULD LIKE TO INFORM YOU THAT, UPON AGREEMENT BETWEEN THE WARRING PARTIES, THE EXCHANGE OF PRISONERS OF WAR, ESPECIALLY THE SERIOUSLY WOUNDED, IS TO BE CARRIED OUT IN ACCORDANCE WITH SEVERAL INTERNATIONAL CONVENTIONS, FOR EXAMPLE, ARTICLE 14 OF THE HAGUE CONVENTION OF 1907 CONCERNING THE LAWS AND CUSTOMS OF WAR ON LAND, AND ARTICLES 68 AND 72 OF THE CONVENTION OF 1929 CONCERNING PRISONERS OF WAR. (THE TEXTS OF THE ABOVEMENTIONED ARTICLES AND CONVENTIONS ARE ATTACHED.)

HOWEVER, TAKING INTO CONSIDERATION THE SEVERE AND SYSTEMATIC ABUSE OF INTERNATIONAL NORMS AND CUSTOMS OF WAR, AS WELL AS CORRESPONDING TREATY OBLIGATIONS, BY GERMANY AND HER ALLIES, WE WILL NOT REACT TO ANY PETITIONS REGARDING THIS MATTER, AND WE WILL NOT ENGAGE IN ANY NEGOTIATIONS OR CORRESPONDENCE CONCERNING THE EXCHANGE OF PRISONERS OF WAR WITH GERMANY AND HER ALLIES.

ATTACHMENTS:
GERMAN LIST OF 297 SOVIET PRISONERS OF WAR (ONE LIST)
ROMANIAN LISTS OF 640 SOVIET PRISONERS OF WAR
ITALIAN LIST OF 117 SOVIET PRISONERS OF WAR (14 PAGES)

COMBINED LISTS OF 17 DECEASED SOVIET PRISONERS OF WAR
10 BURIAL MAPS
EXCERPTS FROM THE INTERNATIONAL CONVENTIONS MEN-
TIONED IN THE BODY OF THE LETTER.

There was no Alexey in the new lists. Neither among the prisoners of war, nor among the deceased. *This is a war, Tanya, it's no time to get upset! Go to work, keep your secret, and keep typing day after day:*

TO COMRADE V. M. MOLOTOV:
THE INTERNATIONAL RED CROSS HAS INFORMED US THAT THE BRITISH GOVERNMENT IS ALLOWING THE PURCHASE OF FOOD SUPPLIES IN AFRICA TO BE SENT TO RUSSIAN PRISONERS OF WAR IN GERMANY AND TO BE TRANSPORTED ON THE SHIPS OF THE INTERNATIONAL RED CROSS. THE FUNDS NEC-ESSARY FOR THESE PURCHASES CAN BE ADVANCED BY THE ICRC BANK OF INTERNATIONAL TRANSACTIONS IN BASEL.

THE INTERNATIONAL RED CROSS ASKS US TO SEND THEM OUR THOUGHTS ON THIS MATTER. I ASSUME, BASED ON YOUR DECISION CONCERNING THE RECENT OFFER TO DISTRIBUTE SUGAR AMONG RUSSIAN PRISONERS OF WAR IN GERMANY AND ROMANIA (SEE ATTACHMENT), WE NEED NOT RESPOND TO THE NEW OFFER FROM ICRC.

VYSHINSKY

+

In 1943, the Vatican again approached the USSR with a proposal to alleviate the suffering of the prisoners of war. This time, the Vatican letter was sent through the USA. Molotov responded:

MOSCOW
28 MARCH 1943

ESTEEMED MR. AMBASSADOR,
WHILE CONFIRMING RECEIPT OF YOUR LETTER OF 25 MARCH OF THIS YEAR CONTAINING THE VATICAN INITIATIVE TO ESTABLISH AN EXCHANGE OF INFORMATION REGARDING SOVIET PRISONERS OF WAR AND PRISONERS OF WAR FROM THE AXIS POWERS, I MUST RESPECTFULLY INFORM YOU THAT AT PRESENT THE SOVIET GOVERNMENT IS NOT INTERESTED IN THIS INITIATIVE.

I EXTEND MY GRATITUDE TO THE US GOVERNMENT FOR THEIR ATTENTION TO SOVIET PRISONERS OF WAR AND ASK YOU, MR. AMBASSADOR, TO ACCEPT THE ASSURANCE OF MY HIGHEST REGARDS.

V. MOLOTOV

In that same year, Molotov explained to the Americans that, from the point of view of propaganda, it would be wrong to represent Germany as capable of any humanitarian actions.

"Why did they behave like that?"

"Who?"

"Molotov and all those people."

"I think they acted in accordance with their position."

"What kind of a position was that—not to rescue their own soldiers who'd been captured?"

"I'd like to know myself. They probably thought: It's all Germany's fault! The Germans signed the Geneva Convention, which states that the care of prisoners of war falls to the side that captured them (even if the other side isn't a member of the Geneva Convention). The Soviet Union believed that Germany should be responsible for our prisoners of war. It's important to understand that the USSR and Germany, neither of whom trusted anyone, hadn't seen any use for international agreements for a long time. You must understand, Sasha, that international agreements work only when you can be punished for not observing them. And who could punish the USSR or Germany? But I've digressed too much again . . . I think you asked why they arrested me?"

"Yes."

It happened rather suddenly. Suddenly and at the same time triumphantly. Following the Victory, the Chekists came for me. We were happy thinking that Asya's dad would come home any day now, but it suddenly became clear that this Victory wasn't ours. A new, personal, but no less destructive war lay ahead of us.

I was arrested in June of 1945. Soviet citizens were living through a very jubilant time, and the Chekists came to my home to the accompaniment of victory marches.

They came at midnight. Tatyana Alexeyevna had just put Asya to bed. There were three of them—the same bigmouthed Soviet hatchlings she'd seen when she first moved to Moscow.

One was left to watch her, while the remaining two—a sweet pair—began vandalizing her apartment.

"Get ready!" one man said calmly, picking his teeth.

"How long will we be gone? I'll ask my neighbor to watch my daughter."

"The girl will go with you. Wake her up!"

Maybe this is good, Tatyana Alexeyevna thought. She went over to her daughter's bed and tried to wake her up. She was stroking the girl's cheek when she noticed one of the Chekists was collecting her drawings.

"What can I take with me?"

"Something warm. And for the child too."

Maybe it's all good? At least they're allowing me to be with Asya. They're Soviet people. The other two are mean, but this one is nice. He still hadn't managed to remove the thing that was between his teeth.

"Can I take this with me?"

"Yes, and take this too."

They allow you to pack your own bag, and so you think, shaking with fear, that these people are humane. They're arresting you, but they're allowing you to take a warm sweater. What good people! It's a delusion. The truth was that the state was unable to provide warm clothes for all those they'd arrested.

Wow, I thought, that's some machine! After all these years, they finally found me. Great job! They'd put so much effort into that paperwork. The perseverance of those people was enviable. Think about it, they found me in 1945!

Tatyana Alexeyevna packed rather quickly. For another half hour, she, with Asya in her arms, watched how the two grown-up men were ripping open comforters and throwing feathers out of the pillows. It might have all looked funny if it wasn't so terrifying. Around two o'clock in the morning, the car finally left the courtyard.

Through the car window, Tatyana saw the dark buildings and thought they were going to prison. Asya was sleeping in her arms, and Tatyana Alexeyevna thought that after a short interrogation, they'd be released so they could sleep. She felt lucky they'd allowed her to keep her child with her—she believed she was ready for anything else.

They'd barely gone three blocks when the car suddenly stopped. Their work was well-coordinated: the man sitting silently in the front passenger seat during the drive abruptly jumped out of the car and opened the back door. The man sitting next to Tatyana grabbed her child and ran in the direction of a bus that was crammed with frightened children. Tatyana began screaming and tried to get out of the car, but she was hit on the back of her head.

"How can you do this? What makes you think you can behave like this? You should act like Soviet citizens and not traumatize children."

I tried to get away, but now the man who first opened the back door got in the car and began strangling me. I felt my pupils dilate. "Mommy!" screamed Asya, and I tried to scream her name, but the Chekist covered my mouth. "Enough of this screaming already! Relax! Nothing will happen to her! The State will take care of her! We'll talk to you now, you'll tell us everything, and you'll be free to go home. And wipe the blood off, don't stain the car!"

They didn't even allow us to say goodbye.

Tatyana Alexeyevna tried to calm down. She thought if she behaved meekly, these people would have pity on her. She later learned that the Chekists called such behavior "the bunny syndrome." You should never try to trust a wolf.

Half an hour later, they arrived at the Lubyanka prison and threw her in a cell.

I remember I was shaking badly. From fear. For Asya. Where are they taking her? What orphanage? How long would they keep me? Could my daughter survive without me for two or three days? Did they take her clothes? No, because I think all the clothes were with me . . . Maybe they can take them to her later?

Dream on! Two or three days! It's funny! An entire week went by before they even started my interrogation. They were working on someone else. The interrogator was too busy for me. Busy. Yep, it truly was a big business!

When they put her in the interrogation chair, with her hands tied, she was completely exhausted. She lifted her head and suddenly started laughing. After one week in a prison cell, the interrogator made her laugh just by the way he looked.

A man with the last name of Kavokin . . . I've remembered him all my life. Even Alzheimer's won't erase that creature from my memory.

He was a small, miserable-looking, balding man of about forty. He wasn't even a man but a mole, that's how faceless he was. He talked in short, abrupt phrases, and drawled a bit.

I think this man must have walked home from work many times in his life and been the target of jokes from the local kids. Kavokin naturally needed to be an interrogator. Only the opportunity to torture other people could give this nonentity some peace. Later in the Gulag, I came to understand that this entire system, this huge machine, was built on insecure, miserable people like him. Individually, those creatures couldn't be taken seriously, but they became important in a government filled with people like them.

It began with a questionnaire. Kavokin asked about her parents, about living abroad, and about other incriminating aspects of her past. He then explained to her that she'd been arrested for a reason, that they don't arrest people without a reason. After an hour of senseless questions, the interrogator suddenly pulled out a pile of her drawings, and the real hourslong interrogation began:

"Did you draw this?"

"Yes."

"What for?"

"What do you mean?"

"What was the purpose of drawing Moscow streets with such precision?"

"These are ordinary drawings. I like drawing."

"And this?"

What could I say? I was sitting with my hands tied. There was a desk, a chair, and a lamp in front of me. The interrogator was waving my drawing of the NKID building in the air, and I think, Gosh, what kind of idiot was I to sketch an official Soviet institution?

Kavokin keeps asking basically the same questions, "What did you draw it for? And this one? And this one here? And the Kremlin?"

I was trying not to annoy him by answering calmly, but it was all going badly. First, he still looked funny to me, and second, he didn't care about my answers anyway.

After about two hours, he moved to the next question:

"Did you send your drawings to your husband?"

"Where?"

"Have you received letters from your husband?"

"Yes, at the very beginning of the war."

"At the very beginning means what year?"

"It began in 1941, in case you've forgotten."

"Don't you dare be rude to me! And after that? Did you receive any letters after that?"

"No, nothing after that. Only at the very beginning of the war, and only two letters."

"Did you know that your husband had defected to the enemy side?"

"No."

"You know now."

"Alexey couldn't have defected to the enemy side. I'm sure Alexey would never have done that. My husband was always a true communist."

"It's not for you, bitch, to decide who's a true communist and who isn't! Is that clear?!"

Wow, I thought, that's quite a transformation! This nonentity can even scream! By that time, I had managed to calm myself down, and now I felt no fear in front of this man behind the desk.

Had anyone ever told him how ridiculous he was?

Kavokin was still yelling something, but Tatyana Alexeyevna had stopped listening to him. She'd lost interest. She was look-ing at this man spitting saliva and recalled her father's last words: "Be brave, Tanya, but don't be foolish. Don't put your head on the chopping block. Be smart and don't be afraid to step back. Be wise! Be capable of agreeing and backing down. Don't try to prove you're brave to a man with a knife. Always be quiet. Don't try to explain to a fool that he's a fool because you can't tell a tree that it's a tree. Don't grumble, moan, or whine. And always be a commonsense centrist!"

"Pavkova! Pavkova! Pavkova, look at me!"

"Yes . . ."

"Yes, Citizen Warden!"

"Yes, Citizen Warden."

"Pavkova, has your husband, Alexey Pavkov, tried to contact you in the last few weeks?"

"What?"

Only at that moment did she realize why they'd arrested her! *Lyosha is alive!*

Several years later, she would repeat those words. They arrested her not because *they'd* found that old list, but because they'd freed her husband.

"Has your husband tried to contact you in the last few weeks?"

I knew from the reports from our agents that when the Americans entered the German POW camps, they recommended to the Russian soldiers that they not return home because it was likely they'd be greeted, not by relatives and friends, but by filtration camps and the Gulag. "They scare our soldiers with torture and interrogations," a Soviet agent reported, "and then they strongly recommend that they have a talk with representatives of the American diplomatic mission."

So that's why they arrested me! He was alive! Alive! Alive! Lyosha was alive! They found me not because of that Romanian list, but only because, I suddenly realized, somewhere, far, far away, my husband had been freed from a POW camp!

You wouldn't believe it, Sasha, but I was so happy to know my husband was alive that I almost hugged that despicable Kavokin.

"Pavkova!"

"Yes . . ."

"Yes, Citizen Warden!"

"Yes, Citizen Warden."

"So, I'm asking you, bitch, has your husband contacted you or not?"

"No."

Kavokin continued screaming, and Tatyana Alexeyevna felt something inexplicable. An intensity of feeling she couldn't compare with anything else. A surge of emotions.

Probably only drugs could have produced such an effect. But who there would have given me even a glass of water? All at once, I experienced feelings of fear and physical pain, anxiety from being apart from my daughter, and happiness from getting my husband back. I didn't know what my pulse rate was, but I was asking my heart just one thing, "Please, don't stop!" The interrogator continued barking, and I couldn't believe my happiness.

"Does this mean it's true?"

"What's true?"

"Does it mean you've arrested me because Alexey is alive?"

"Your husband, you filthy traitor, has been arrested because he defected to the enemy, and I'm the one asking the questions!"

"Alive! That means he's truly alive!" She was jubilant.

I didn't know what would happen to me in an hour, I didn't know what would happen to my daughter or to my husband the next day, but at that first interrogation, I was happy that, despite everything, our family had survived the war.

It was very silly, don't you think? A man is transferred from one Titanic to another but doesn't realize it and so feels happy because he's not at the bottom of the ocean yet. I can't recall those minutes precisely, but after another question from the interrogator, I think I burst into laughter.

"Did I say something funny, you bitch?"

"No, not you, Citizen Warden, but fate."

I'm not sure all this found its way into the transcript. I don't think he even kept a transcript. The interrogator couldn't have cared less about my answers, or about my laughter and tears.

"Get out of here!"

That was how the first interrogation ended. The conversation was suddenly interrupted, and the prisoner was escorted back to her cell.

It seemed to me that the fact everything had ended so quickly, that Kavokin had sent me away so soon, could mean only one thing—he realized I was innocent. During that long, dark night, I couldn't fall asleep—I believed the worst was over. What an idiot!

The next evening, Kavokin again summoned Pavkova for interrogation. She waited a long time as he wrote something down, and then when he was finally done, she said with a smile:

"Good evening, Citizen Warden!"
"Who allowed you to speak, bitch?"
"What happened to my daughter?" I asked.
"I'll ask you again, you filthy traitor: who allowed you to speak?"
"Listen, why are you talking to me like that?"

That was a mistake. Kavokin hit her. Tatyana thought the interrogator had knocked her tooth loose, and she covered her mouth with her hand. Kavokin was a small man and looked weak, but he had a good punch. The long years of training had not been wasted.

"Did you know, you ugly cow, that your husband was captured?"

Kavokin asked this question calmly, and she thought for a second—why does he constantly change from informal to formal modes of address? Why does he sometimes scream, then sometimes appear to listen to her?

"I didn't know it for sure, but I assumed . . ."

"Based on what facts could you assume this?"

"When his letters stopped coming, I wanted to believe that he hadn't died but was captured."

"So, you filthy bitch, you wanted to believe your husband was a traitor?"

"I'm sure my husband always fought bravely."

"Brave soldiers don't get captured!"

"I think there are different situations. It's possible to be surrounded by the enemy . . ."

"You can still kill yourself with your last bullet!"

"Even if we assume for a second that he didn't do that, what does it have to do with me?"

"What do you mean, what does it have to be with you? You're his wife, you bitch!"

"Since when does the wife of a suspect become a defendant?"

"Since it was written in the Soviet Constitution, which you must respect, you cunt!"

"I respect the Soviet Constitution," she answered calmly, "but I still don't understand why I have to answer for my husband's actions."

"Because your marriage is proof of a conspiracy!"

"Are you serious?"

"What are you trying to say, bitch, that you got married without any preliminary conspiracy? This isn't Tsarist Russia—in the Soviet Union people get married for love, and therefore, you scum, you must have known that you'd fallen in love with the enemy!"

It was all so ridiculous! I began laughing again and, it seems, this finally got to the interrogator. But before I drove him into a total rage, I managed to pour some oil on the fire. I burst out laughing again and asked him:

"Listen, you must realize that everything you're saying here is complete nonsense! Plus, on top of everything, you look very funny. What are you going to do? Hit me again?"

Yes, he was.

"So, it's all funny to you? Funny, huh? Kolya, come here!"

Kavokin jumped up from behind his desk, ran toward Tatyana, and hit her again. She tried to get up, but someone behind her back put his hands on her shoulders.

"This is all funny to you, huh, you bitch?! We'll see how funny you find it now!"

Kavokin began unbuckling his belt and opening his fly. Tatyana closed her eyes. Something was touching her face, but she didn't want to imagine what it was.

The person behind her lifted Tatyana Alexeyevna up and threw her on the floor. A heavy man sat on top of her and pulled up her dress. Kavokin tried to penetrate her, but he couldn't. He groaned, tried to arouse himself, but nothing worked . . . for several days.

Every night Interrogator Kavokin summoned Tatyana Pavkova to the interrogation chamber and tried to rape her. For four days, he couldn't accomplish it, so he beat her up instead. Finally, at the end of the fourth day, he collapsed onto his chair and ordered his assistant to "do it." The assistant obeyed.

+

HOSPITAL CHART
PAVKOVA, TATYANA ALEXEYEVNA
35 years old
Russian
Literate
Married
Place of birth: London
Admission Diagnosis
11 July
The patient was admitted complaining of lightheadedness, pain throughout her body, and vomiting. The patient is of medium height, standard build, and satisfactorily nourished; her visible mucous membranes and skin are extremely pale. Her position in bed is prone; she cannot turn over by herself. An examination has revealed hematomas on the hips, buttocks, lower back, and all the way up to the bottom of both shoulder blades. The hematomas are of a homogeneous dark-purple color. Her right hand is swollen, and there is a hematoma on the back of it. Her tongue is clear, her stomach is soft. The patient's general condition is critical. The patient is delirious, she moans and calls for her husband and daughter. According to the patient, there has been no urination or defecation for two days. Her pulse rate is 70.

13 July
The patient's condition is critical. Not capable of turning in bed without help. Vomiting has stopped. There was no stool. Urination occurs with difficulty.

15 July

The same.

16 July

Complains of headache. She can lift her right hand with difficulty. The swelling has slightly decreased.

17 July

The patient can turn slightly. Her overall condition is slightly improved. The difficulty urinating has passed.

20 July

The swelling of the right hand is gone. Freedom of movement is restored.

21 July

Overall condition is satisfactory. Can turn on her own. Complains of headaches.

23 July

The same.

25 July

After the last night of interrogation at 1:45 A.M., the patient was released from a rope. There is a slightly pronounced strangulation furrow on the patient's neck. The pulse is satisfactory.

29 July

Overall condition is satisfactory. The appearance of the visible mucous membranes and skin is pale.

1 August

The patient's overall condition is improving. Note: poor appetite and lower back pain.

3 August

No noticeable changes.

5 August

Overall condition is satisfactory.

+

Her overall condition is satisfactory—so the patient can be discharged. The investigation is over. After being raped, a completely exhausted Tatyana Alexeyevna was sent to the prison hospital. When the orderlies decided she was ready, she was again sent for interrogation. This time Kavokin didn't say anything, but his assistant went straight to the point. Now there was only one thing she didn't understand—how that man could have agreed to rape a basically living corpse. When she returned to the hospital, she attempted suicide, but the orderlies came just in time to cut off the sheet. With this, the criminal investigation ended. She was convicted to fifteen years and, as soon as her health allowed, she was placed on the Stolypin prisoner transport. Get ready, sweetie, for a month-long journey. By the way, we wanted to ask you: How's your mood now? Is everything all right? Not funny anymore?

Before her departure, in a crystal-clear manner, the interrogator Kavokin described her future: "Your husband, you louse, will be executed (if he hasn't already been), your daughter will be sent to an orphanage, and if, after fifteen years, by some crazy chance, you happen to meet, she probably won't recognize you. You can be sure our educators will take care of that."

"We'll see," Pavkova said hoarsely, gazing at him from under her brows.

The train stuffed with the wives of enemies of the people started off on that cross-country journey to the labor camps. The women told each other the stories of their interrogations, but Tatyana Alexeyevna didn't open her eyes. The scariest thing on the journey turned out to be the stops. When the train slowed down, she thought she'd scream. For the first week, then the second, she dreamt only about the train reaching its final destination. By the twentieth day, death seemed like an escape. She sat pressed against the wall and whispered the lines of Barto's poem:

His house, which once had stood right there,
Right on that very spot,
Had now completely disappeared!
Poor Syoma was distraught!

"Where is building number four?"
Cried Syoma in alarm.
"I cannot see it anymore!"
Syoma said to the gendarme.

"I'm now back from the Crimea,
With no home to shelter me!
Where is that big grey house of mine
Where Mama used to be?"

Upon their arrival, they were brought to the edge of a pit. Some of the women began screaming and throwing themselves into the pit even before any shots were fired. Tatyana Alexeyevna was quiet.

It's amazing, I thought, that someone can still have a fear of death. If at that moment someone had offered me a bullet, I would have gladly taken it . . . just like the pill from that Italian doctor many years ago. Was it really me who back then cried over a ball of snot?

After a month on the train, she was absolutely indifferent to where she would go—to the barracks or the grave.

Plus, I hated myself. I couldn't forgive myself for my breakdown in prison. My husband was in the Gulag, my daughter had been taken to an orphanage, but I was thinking only about myself. I stood on that precipice without any fear of death. I was ready to die not so much from fatigue but from shame.

Unfortunately, there were no shots. We stood there for half an hour, and then they herded us away. As it turned out, those were their favorite jokes. All the new prisoners were put through that show. You know how much they loved theater in the Soviet Union . . . especially anatomical theater.

When they arrived at the labor camp, they were lined up on both sides of a sandy road. When everyone had finally taken their place, a deadly silence descended—the guards began walking between the rows of women. Like shoppers in a supermarket, they made their way down the rows.

I think for the first time in my thirty-plus years of life I was happy I wasn't pretty. I understood that most likely no one would choose me of their own volition. It all reminded me of an audition at a movie studio or of a fancy-dress ball. The women were dressed in the clothes they had been arrested in: Some had suit jackets over their nightgowns, others were wearing tattered evening gowns. I remember when I was telling Yadviga this story, my friend suddenly stopped me:

"Wait!" she argued, "that's not possible! How could they have only nightgowns on? They'd been in prison for months, and tossed around on trains for weeks before that . . . How could they have lived through all that in a nightgown?"

As if anyone cared:

The State provided clothes only in the Gulag. That first night

*we were taken into a closet-like room and offered a choice of
footwear. There was a pile of new boots in front of us, but in
only one size, thirty-seven.*

"Don't like it—go barefoot."

After the "beauty pageant" and the "golden shoe award,"
they were finally housed in their new "living quarters" called
octets. They were former factory blocks with neither windows
nor floors. There was straw on the ground and mud on the roof.
The buildings were called octets because the temperature inside
never rose above the number that looks like a vertical infinity
sign.[3] There wasn't even cold water in summer. In winter, they
melted snow to make tea or took water from an ice-hole, where
from time to time the desperate ones drowned themselves.

*The women surrounded the overseer. They bombarded her
with questions about the living conditions, the food, and the
daily schedule.*

*I was totally indifferent, but still I could understand these
women who were trying to organize their lives somehow. They
asked all those questions to get some whiff of hope:*

"This won't be terrible, and this, girls, isn't so bad . . ."

*I turned toward the wall and tried to fall asleep, but without
much success. After prison, the hospital, and three and a half
weeks on a train, my body was wracked with pain. The conditions of the Soviet prisoner transport were hardly suitable for
healing the wounds left by the interrogations.*

+

[3] 8 degrees Celsius is approximately 46 degrees Fahrenheit. [Translators'
note]

Tatyana Alexeyevna continues her story, and I closely examine the paintings. This time, my eye catches the portrait of a man. Familiar gray colors, cold as the canvas. Once again, there's a bright light, but this time it's coming from a desk lamp. Behind the desk, there's a man, small but very scary. His mouth is slightly opened, and I can see his sharp crooked teeth. It feels like this man is about to attack me.

It was two months since I'd heard anything about Asya. After several weeks on the train, I learned that they made arrangements with orphanages first, and only then did they arrest the mothers. The complicated system of Soviet communication. Waiting for a new group of children to arrive, the orphanage directors could surmise that there were going to be arrests. But this isn't entirely accurate. The orphanage directors waited for 'new arrivals' every day, so they stopped thinking about the constant arrests. This country, which was already filled with street children, couldn't give up its terrible habit of producing orphans even after the war was over.

I understood that the most important thing was to survive the first year in the camp. An organism can adapt to anything. I needed to give myself a year, maybe two. There are certain things that are important in life; the rest is trivial. The most important thing was that at some point we—Lyosha, Asya, and I—would all be together . . .

For the few first weeks, I collected cattail, just like everybody else. On the fourteenth day, a miracle happened—I was sum-moned to the warden's office.

"Pavkova," he asked, "is it true you worked at the NKID?"

"Yes, it's true," I answered.

"Well, sit down at the typewriter!" The warden's suggestion seemed so strange to me that I didn't move.

"Why are you standing there? Sit down!"

I was at a loss, but I understood that I shouldn't let this opportunity pass. It was warm in his office—you could only dream of a job like that!

I sat down. The warden gave me a notebook and ordered me to retype a list that was divided into columns.

"With all the formatting?" I asked, trying to lend more signif-icance to my actions.

"Type as you like, as you did it back in Moscow . . ."

INFORMATION
CONCERNING CHILD MORTALITY IN THE LABOR CAMPS
DURING THE FIRST HALF OF 1945

TOTAL NUMBER OF DEAD --

IN ABSOLUTE INDICATORS --

IN RELATIVE INDICATORS --

PERCENT DISTRIBUTION OF MORTALITY AMONG SPECIFIC
TYPES OF ILLNESSES --

MORTALITY BY MONTH AND ACCORDING TO DIAGNOSED
ILLNESSES --

"Good, Pavkova, that's enough! I'll arrange everything—you can begin tomorrow."

She got lucky. The warden of the labor camp, a man with the last name of Podushkin (from *podushka*, or 'pillow') was in fact lazy and conniving. He knew it was a crime to entrust an enemy of the people with such documentation, but the pretty young thing he'd placed in the job couldn't handle it. She couldn't deal with official documents and made tons of mistakes in the letters she managed to type. Lines jumped and letters disappeared, just as people did all over the country. It took Tatyana Alexeyevna several weeks to organize the mess she'd inherited.

THERE ARE REPORTS THAT SOME LABOR CAMP NURSING STATIONS AND THE DEPARTMENT OF CORRECTIONAL AND LABOR COLONIES OFTEN USE THE DIAGNOSIS "EXHAUSTION" IN THE DEATH CERTIFICATES THEY ISSUE.

WHEN THE COURTS THAT DELIVERED THE CONVICTIONS AND THE RELATIVES OF THE DECEASED SEE THESE CERTIFICATES, SUCH A DIAGNOSIS PROVOKES UNWANTED CONCLUSIONS ABOUT THE CAUSE OF DEATH.

THEREFORE, IT IS NECESSARY:

TO GIVE NOT ONLY THE PRIMARY DIAGNOSIS BUT ALSO SECONDARY DIAGNOSES (CARDIAC ARREST, DECREASE OF HEART ACTIVITY, TUBERCULOSIS, AND SO FORTH) WHEN DOCUMENTING DEATH FROM EXHAUSTION.

IN CERTIFICATES THAT ARE TO BE SENT FROM THE CAMP TO VARIOUS ORGANIZATIONS AND TO THE OFFICE OF VITAL STATISTICS OF THE NKVD, ONLY SECONDARY DIAGNOSES SHOULD BE SPECIFIED.

LEAVE THE PRIMARY DIAGNOSIS IN THE MEDICAL STATISTICAL REPORTS THE CAMP SENDS TO THE GULAG'S MEDICAL DEPARTMENT.

INSTRUCTIONS
REGARDING THE PROCEDURE FOR REMOVING
GOLD DENTURES FROM DECEASED PRISONERS:

- GOLD DENTURES ARE SUBJECT TO REMOVAL FROM DECEASED PRISONERS.
- THE REMOVAL OF GOLD DENTURES SHOULD BE CONDUCTED

IN THE PRESENCE OF A SPECIAL COMMITTEE CONSISTING OF REPRESENTATIVES OF MEDICAL SERVICES, THE CAMP ADMINISTRATION, AND THE FINANCIAL DEPARTMENT.

- UPON REMOVAL OF GOLD DENTURES, THE COMMITTEE SHOULD WRITE A REPORT (TWO COPIES) SPECIFYING THE EXACT NUMBER OF UNITS EXTRACTED (CROWNS, TEETH, HOOKS, CLASTS, ETC.) AND THEIR WEIGHT.

- THE REPORT IS TO BE SIGNED BY ALL THE ABOVE-MENTIONED OFFICIALS. ONE COPY SHALL REMAIN IN THE ARCHIVE OF THE CAMP'S MEDICAL DEPARTMENT; A SECOND COPY, ALONG WITH THE EXTRACTED GOLD DENTURES, SHALL BE TRANSFERRED TO THE CAMP'S FINANCIAL DEPARTMENT.

- THE GOLD OBTAINED SHALL BE DEPOSITED IN THE NEAREST DESIGNATED BRANCH OF THE STATE BANK, AND THE RECEIPT FOR THE GOLD DEPOSITED IN THE STATE BANK SHOULD BE ATTACHED TO THE FIRST COPY OF THE REPORT.

I learned a lot in the first month. I now knew that in the event a prisoner eats a dog or a cat, it should be reported as gross misconduct. It was important to explain to Moscow that the convict had done it only as a prank, as there was no hunger in the camp. But my boss comforted me, telling me not to worry about the animals—as everything living (excluding people) had been eaten a long time ago. Only several years later was I fully able to appreciate his strange sense of humor. My boss was not joking when he alluded to cannibalism. As soon as the first snow fell and the ground froze, they stopped burying the prisoners' corpses, despite the official burial instructions and the constant directives from the capital, and began stacking them behind one of the barracks.

"Let them come here and dig the graves themselves, if they want!" Podushkin said indignantly as he drank his tea from the saucer. "Crazy bunch! If those Moscow types are so smart, what

do they propose? That we gather all the convicts and have them dig the graves? That's fine with me, but what's the point? By the time they dig through this hellish ground to bury such a huge number of dead bodies, half the diggers will be dead! It's a vicious circle, and I have a tree logging quota to think about!"

From time to time, fresh corpses would be missing body parts. As a rule, everyone would turn a blind eye. In those rare cases when, for some reason, they had to issue an explanation, Tatyana Alexeyevna would blame it on wolves, which had never been seen in the vicinity.

Sometimes the warden, after getting sufficiently drunk, would put on a show. He'd take a shovel, put a piece of rotten meat on it, and go out into the prison yard. Every female convict could leave the barracks and crawl on her hands and knees to the shovel to bite off as much meat as she could. I remember how my colleague, the warden's brainless lover, said mournfully, "God, how low can a human being fall!"

You'd think she was talking about her lover, but no, she was talking about those exhausted women. I remained silent. Nothing out of the ordinary was happening. Those people (I'm referring here to people, not to that pervert in charge) behaved logically and rationally. The women—mothers, daughters, and sisters—were trying to save their own lives. There was nothing extraordinary in their behavior, and it certainly wasn't a sign of the decay of the human race. Other things, however, were rather more surprising. I understood that the experiment—the creation of a new man—that had been launched by the great architect of human souls was moving ahead at full speed. The scariest thing, I thought, was not that exhausted prisoners were trying to bite a piece of meat, but the idea that, if we didn't change anything, if the world never learned about these atrocities, then, half a century later, a process of crystallization would take place, resulting in human beings who would eat from a shovel of their own free will. And if that difficult realization never took place, and if the powers-that-be did not repent, then human beings would stand in line to eat from a shovel full of pancakes, and they would be happy, they would be ecstatic to eat from the shovel, because their prison would no longer be the Gulag but their own selves.

Despite her "good position," Tatyana Alexeyevna still didn't know anything about her daughter. Even proximity to the administration didn't help. All her requests were answered with the same curt "No." She wanted to believe that life was tolerable in the orphanage. She hoped that her daughter, if possible, was not too homesick. On the other hand, Tatyana Alexeyevna was glad that Asya couldn't see her.

She continued reflecting on the idea that Soviet forced-labor camps were a grand experiment, a special laboratory, and a powerful mathematical equation, which would result in a new Soviet man. But the more she reflected on the matter, the more she realized it was nonsense.

If we were all units in that equation, if all of us convicts were just a part of some formula, then we'd all have to live by the same set of rules. But that wasn't happening. Not at all! There were millions of mistakes! Chaos was the only known 'given.' There was pure, absolute chaos in our camp. Some women were allowed to write letters to their husbands, others were not. Among those convicted under the same article, some were sent to the camp with their children; others, like me, attempted for years to connect with their families. I wasn't allowed to inquire about what had happened to my own daughter, while there were convicts in our barracks who were allowed visits. But, at times, I thought it was all for the best, as I wasn't sure I was strong enough to see Asya. In our block, there was a woman who went insane after an hour-long visit with her son. Quite literally. When the five-year boy saw his exhausted mother with gray hair, he had hugged his grandma and asked, "Will Mommy always be so ugly?"

Every day for the next two years, that woman sat in front of her small mirror, covered with cracks, and prepared for her son's next visit. Two years of preparing and beautifying herself ended up in an all-expenses-paid trip to the insane asylum. I watched that poor mother and recalled Asya and her gentle little hands, hoping that one day she'd forgive me. I realized that at that very moment my little girl was falling asleep in an orphanage, and I wanted to die from the feeling of my own powerlessness. I was so ashamed of myself. I closed my eyes and tried to recall our ordinary evenings together in Moscow. I was ready to condemn myself for taking Asya to kindergarten. Asya was crying and the teachers were hissing at me. I obeyed them and left, thinking it would be better for everyone. Excommunicated from love. One shouldn't have any attachments. You'll soon grow up, my dear, and you'll have to live alone. Tenderness was rationed out, and love was distributed by quota. In the evenings, we would wrap ourselves around each other like the roots of the same tree and bask in our closeness. Asya would smile at me, but the next morning I'd take her back to kindergarten and leave. Asya would cry and the teachers would whisper to me, "Leave, your daughter should be left alone . . ."

When Tatyana Alexeyevna couldn't fall asleep on her bunk, she thought that Asya had foreseen their separation. Children always sense forthcoming disasters.

Asya was always telling me, "Mom, I want to give you a hug, Mom, don't leave, I want to give you a kiss!" But all that just seemed like beautiful silliness.

"We'll have enough time for kisses!" I'd answer.

"When?"

I would stroke her cheek and go to work . . .

Sometimes if I came home tired, I would bark at Asya. It was *fairly common. I'd yell not because my daughter was guilty of anything, but only because I'd had a hard day. What mother hasn't experienced that? Back then, all that seemed ordinary and understandable. Now, I couldn't forgive myself. Just like all the women around me, I'd burst into tears every time I thought about the kind look in Asya's eyes. We asked our children for forgiveness but didn't know if they'd ever hear us. I tried to fall asleep and saw a little girl who wasn't guilty of anything but was ready to apologize for everything she hadn't done if only her mother wouldn't be mad at her.*

You know, Sasha, I understood over the years that the relationship between Soviet citizens and Stalin was built on the same principle. A strict father is loved in spite of everything. Even here in the camp, after losing relatives and friends, women dreamed of being warmly embraced by the leader. Like little children who would stop at nothing to earn their father's good will, they wanted to smooth over their own guilt before their tired parents. Firm but fair? No, that's not the case! He's your father, and therefore it's not important what kind of father he is. You don't get to choose your relatives. The leader was becoming a given, the first among equals, a superhuman who, like Adam, was supposed to live nine hundred years. Stalin's genius lay in his ability to convince millions of people of their kinship. Sometimes when I thought about him, I recalled the words of my own father. Dad liked to repeat that there is no god. And if there is no god, then no one is responsible. What can you expect from such people? They're not creations of a higher power, but just a biological species. Slightly smarter than a donkey, and slightly sneakier than a cat. Misfortunes befall us only because we're imperfect. We're not dolphins, not even dogs. There's nothing to discuss here—we're just too stupid!

I tried to obey my father's words, and I agreed with him on many things. Yes, you know, Sasha, I realize now that there, in the camp, I understood my father and agreed with him about everything . . . well, almost everything.

I can't remember if I told you that my father was an atheist. For a long time, I was an atheist too, just like my father, but in the camp . . . the camp made me believe in God.

"How?"

How? It's very simple! God became a means of self-help. God became my salvation. God became a resource and a way to organize my life. He became my experience and the matter produced by my brain. We were not given any pills, I couldn't buy valerian root or vodka, but I could invent a god who would help me. In my head I found a corner, some cells that were responsible for what we called God, and I turned them on, and they helped me not to lose my mind. I turned on the mechanism of God in my head, and that mechanism worked. There it wasn't important whether God really existed or not; what was important was that I could reach him and use him for my own salvation. God was my neurologist. God was my understanding of my own abilities. Everything that was going on in the camp was so stupid, so cruel, and so screwed up that only the existence of a Supreme Being could comfort me. Nietzsche proclaimed that God was dead. In response, Dostoevsky complained that if God didn't exist, then everything was permitted, but I thought exactly the opposite. Only the existence of God could justify everything that was happening to us. Evil had been created not by the absence of God but by God's will. The abyss that swallowed men after all the bridges had collapsed could only be explained by divine design, not by evolution. There was something important in that design. There was no nature in it, but there was a secret, and that secret was mine alone. I didn't know of any animals, other than humans, that could find enjoyment in torture, and I longed for the day when I could confront a divine being who would have to answer for all this. I had to create a god in my head, a god that I could visit one day to demand an explanation. I saw how the guards enjoyed our suffering, and I felt that somewhere, high in the sky, there must be a god encouraging this evil. Only a creator designed by me, only a demiurge that was necessary for me, could serve as a justification for those monstrous designs. There, in the camps, they didn't want to annihilate us, they wanted to torture us. They tested us in the same way fabrics are tested for durability. They killed women not on command but by chance. And there was no great experiment in all that, but there was suffering, and there was nothing human in it, but there was God. When I was typing the lists of those who'd died from a common cold, I realized that I needed someone I could call to account. And I didn't make copies of those documents for myself, but I kept locked in my memory everything that I could charge him with on the day of that most important reckoning, scarier than the Last Judgement. Not the warden of our camp, not even that pitiful embezzling bandit Stalin, were of any concern to me. I needed a god, because I realized that only He would be able truly to answer for all this. I knew that I couldn't reach Stalin, and the thought of avenging myself against the leader brought me no comfort; only the possibility of avenging myself against God kept me going. And I dreamed of slapping God in the face! I wanted to grab his throat, tighten the grip of my boney fingers, and listen to him gasping for air. Believe me, Sasha, there was so much grievance and anger inside me that I would have strangled any god. There was so much wrath in my heart that its power could have stopped the world, and so, to avoid that, I had to create a mighty being, a being capable of taking the blow.

That's why I created him, and that's why I became a believer. Every night, along with some other women, I prayed before small icons, and if someone gave me the opportunity to prove the sincerity of my faith, if it were necessary to die for some piece of wood bearing the image of Jesus or any of the saints, I would have done it without hesitation. Every time I kneeled, I prayed to God for his wellbeing. I asked him not to disappear or vanish. And all those years he reigned in good health only because I was waiting for a letter.

But now, when everything in my life is over, exactly now, that very god that I created has decided to give me Alzheimer's because he's afraid! He's afraid to look me in the eyes! He wants me to forget everything. Alzheimer's interrupts my path to him, and my Alzheimer's is the best proof that he's afraid of me.

I don't know what to say. The scene is ridiculous. It's way past midnight and there's an old lady sitting here with an ornery young guy. And they're talking about God. But what's there to say on the topic? People start talking about God only when there's nothing left to say about people.

"How long were you in the camp?" I ask, getting up from the short stool and stretching my legs.

"Ten years."

"Did they release you early?"

"Yes."

"And after that? Did you see your husband? Did you find your daughter?"

"I'm tired. Let's talk about it tomorrow."

"Tomorrow you won't remember anything."

"Please, Alexander . . . I need to get up early tomorrow!"

I obey. I leave the bag of food, exit onto the staircase landing, and a moment later, I'm home. My apartment is empty and quiet—my second life hasn't had enough time to accumulate stuff. I brush my teeth, turn off the light, and fall onto my new bed.

I have a dream. I'm in a theater. The auditorium is incredibly beautiful, and the audience is well dressed. The acoustics are good, and the conductor quite famous. In the concert program, there's a concerto for a symphony orchestra and . . . for an MRI machine. On stage, where there would typically be a grand piano, there's a white MRI scanner rising up like an iceberg. Lana appears on stage to the sound of applause, wearing not a dress but a man's dinner jacket. She passes the trombones, walks alongside the violas, and, after shaking hands with the first cellist, lies down on the gurney. The audience is quiet.

A man from the percussion section approaches the scanner and pushes the button. Lana slowly disappears inside the machine. The conductor raises his baton, freezes for a moment, and then allows the machine to start. Rapid electrical impulses inside the scanner initiate the vibration of the metal coils. The concerto begins with an MRI solo. We hear a repeated unpleasant knocking sound. In a moment, this sound reaches 125 decibels. The orchestra starts next, but even at its full symphonic strength, the sound of the solo dominates. It's frightening music. Sad and unbearable. The melody of pain. There is sorrow in every note, and in every crash of the percussion, there is death. I don't like this music. I don't want Lana to play it, but the audience seems to like it. With the final chord, the audience bursts into applause. The audience screams "Bravo!" But I keep quiet—I don't want Lana to go into the machine for an encore.

+

Do you need an explanation
Of who he is, the Russian god?
Allow me this brief recitation,
A reflection thereupon.

God of snowstorms, god of ditches,
God of pothole-covered roads,
Post-horse stations filled with roaches,
That is he, the Russian god.

God of beggars at the gates,
God of the hungry, of the cold,
God of unprofitable estates,
That is he, the Russian god.

God of sagging breasts and asses,
Chubby feet and birch-bark shoes,
Bitter cream and sour faces,
That is he, the Russian god.

God of brandies, god of pickles,
God of souls that live in hock,
Provincial morons and the fickle,
That is he, the Russian god.

God of those bedecked with medals,
God of house-serfs barely shod,
Of their masters in their horse sleds,
That is he, the Russian god.

Dunces get a silver spoon,
Those with brains, they get the rod,
God of all that's opportune,
That is he, the Russian god.

God of all that's brightly lustered,
Of all that's odd and from abroad
God of meat before the mustard,
That is he, the Russian god.

God of foreign wanderers
Who plant themselves in Russian sod,
God of dull administrators,
That is he, the Russian god.

Peter Vyazemsky
Moscow, 1828

+

At nine o'clock in the morning, someone rings my doorbell. There are no movers coming today, so I realize it's probably my neighbor. Which is in fact true, only instead of Tatyana Alexeyevna, there's a young woman outside my door.

"Good morning!" the girl says, smiling, and hands me a pie.

"Hello . . ." I respond, rubbing my eyes.

"My name is Lera. I'm your downstairs neighbor. I wanted to meet you."

"This is some city!" I think. "A pretty woman shows up on her own at your door at nine in the morning!"

The woman goes into the kitchen, places the pie on the table, and moves over to the window. I turn on the tea kettle and open the fridge thinking of what else I might offer my guest. As if following some hospitality ritual, my neighbor studies my kitchen for several seconds and then sits down on the windowsill. I place teacups on the table and look out at the courtyard. Outside, in the kindergarten yard, the kids are collecting leaves and piling them under a rusty rocket.

"What do you think—why do they do it?" Lera asks.

"They want to fly away."

"Through the entire galaxy?"

"Over the fence."

There's an uncomfortable pause. I don't know what else to say, and so I decide to try out the new radio that was delivered yesterday with the furniture.

"Is it okay if I turn on some music? I bought this yesterday but haven't had time to check it out."

"Of course, please!"

The radio works. I surf through several radio stations, but when Lera says, "Leave that," I stop. The kids outside continue piling leaves under the rusty rocket.

"I know your story," my neighbor says, suddenly turning off the radio.

"Oh, I see."

"Do you mind if I help you? I've never done it before, but I think I could babysit your daughter. You have a girl, right?"

"Yes," I answer, closing the kitchen window.

"Good! Then I'll come to your place. And don't smoke here! Okay, so we'll see each other tonight?"

"Tonight?"

"Yeah, we could maybe watch a movie."

"Why not."

"Maybe a comedy?"

"Yes, a comedy would be fine."

I see Lera out and follow her onto the landing. I glance at my neighbor's door and notice a new red cross. Now there's one on Tatyana Alexeyevna's door, too.

"Do you know who lives there?" Lera asks.

"Yes, I know," I answer.

"They say she's had a very hard life."

"It's true."

"They say she never found her family."

"How do you know that?"

"The woman who sold you the apartment told me."

"It's not true! It can't be true!"

"I don't know, but I clearly remember that's what she said."

At that moment, my neighbor's door opens. Tatyana Alexeyevna walks out onto the landing.

"Hello, Alexander!"

"Hello!"

"How did you sleep in your new place?"

"Well, thanks! Where are you off to?"

"To Kuropaty. If you'd like, you can come along—we could use some extra people."

"What is it?"

"There's a taxi waiting for me. Are you coming or not?"

"Yes, I'll get ready."

In the taxi, I learn that Kuropaty is the site of a mass grave near Minsk where they buried victims of the Great Terror of the 1930s. Divisions of the NKVD executed tens of thousands of people over there.

"Are your daughter and husband buried there?" I ask, looking through the foggy window at the unfamiliar streets of Minsk.

"No, I don't have anyone buried there."

"Then why are we going there?"

"You moved here recently, right?"

"Yes."

"Then you probably don't know that our authorities decided to demolish Kuropaty and put a highway though the cemetery."

"Can't they put the road somewhere else?"

"Apparently not. Plus, it's important to understand that this is a political moment. Our leader is red to the marrow of his bones. He doesn't like that we're honoring the the victims of the Terror. The custom here is to praise Stalin, not to criticize him. For several months now, people have been guarding the memorial, but the authorities won't back down. They're sending trucks and bulldozers to Kuropaty to demolish the crosses that were recently put up."

"I can't believe that in 2001, after everything we've learned, someone could think of doing that."

"Oh, Sasha! I envy your naiveté! Well, you'll have a chance now to meet those people in person."

When we arrive at the place, I see people carrying national symbols. The police, overwhelming in numbers, are standing opposite them. Tatyana Alexeyevna warns me that half of the demonstrators are Belorussian KGB agents dressed in civilian clothes. "Be careful!"

It's drizzling. The atmosphere is tense. I watch additional police units arrive. Guys dressed in brown camouflage greet their colleagues and smile. Servants of the people. The young men shake each other's hands and casually begin arresting the activists, probably for the sake of their police report. It seems, despite the prevailing tension, the authorities aren't nervous at all, unlike the protesters. What's more, the men in uniform display all the signs of being in a good mood. They're not afraid of the activists and even appear to be enjoying their job. We can hear the song of a local pop group emanating from one of the police cars:

You open doors for me
And I whisper in your ear:
I am your god,
My name is love.

I am your god,
My name is love
If you could believe in me once
You'll believe again and again . . .

There are trucks loaded with sand driving around. A bull-dozer stands nearby. It has probably been assigned to dig up the crosses.

"Tatyana Alexeyevna, I think the guys who are protecting the memorial can get by without you."

"But why? Why wouldn't the police arrest a ninety-year-old woman?"

"You seriously think they'd dare to demolish the crosses?"

"Only if we back down."

Tatyana Alexeyevna gives me a candle. I light it and shelter it with my hand. Up to the last moment, I can't believe that anyone would try to break us up, but after several isolated skirmishes half an hour later, the security forces are getting ready to attack. Their batons are at the ready, their berets visible everywhere. Suddenly we find ourselves surrounded. A muscular giant pushes me. I manage to remain standing, but Tatyana Alexeyevna, when pushed by the same giant, falls to the ground.

"What are you doing, asshole?!"

They drag us through the sand. They don't beat us, just drag us in the direction of the militia vans. I can see that the arrests are still going on behind us, but it's no longer any of my business. I brush the sand off my jacket and smile at Tatyana Alexeyevna.

"These guys don't waste any time. I couldn't understand anything. What did they arrest us for?"

"For coming here to pay our respects to the victims of Stalinist repression."

"Are you okay?"

"Compared to the Soviets, these guys are puppy dogs."

"What will happen now? Will they write an incident report?"

"Yeah. I think they'll accuse us of resisting the security forces."

"Is there a fine?"

"Yeah."

"Damn it! I didn't bring my passport with me."

"That was very foolish of you, Sasha!"

"But you didn't tell me where we were going."

The office is brown. The desk is old. The floor is older than the desk. On the wall, there's a portrait of the president looking solemn and a calendar with stuffed bunnies on it. Two chairs, a dark-blue safe, and a white radio.

> In the blue sky the sun sends down its rays,
> While behind the court walls the investigator weaves his case.
> For whom? For some boy, for no one.
> For whom? For some boy, for no one.

They process us very quickly. The policeman seems preoccupied—he reminds his colleagues that today is his daughter's birthday. Tatyana Alexeyevna explains that I'm a family friend who came to visit. And that I got involved in the protest by accident. With the investigator's permission, I call my mother, and Uncle Grisha brings me my passport. When the militiaman explains the charges to us, Tatyana Alexeyevna laughs:

"Officer, of course, I understand that you need to write a report. Moreover, I'm very grateful that my young companion and I are accused of nothing more than using coarse language. But you see, we have a problem here. Even if we assume that Alexander is capable of swearing, Officer, things are trickier with me—I have Alzheimer's, and I've forgotten all the bad words."

"Tatyana Alexeyevna," the policeman answers calmly after looking down at the form, "Don't mess with me. I've already written the report. Let's not waste my time. I have a truckload of protestors like you waiting for me."

With a sour face, my stepfather asks if we need a ride. I realize that Tatyana Alexeyevna's company will make him uncomfortable, so I instantly agree. At first, we're just trying to warm up and so don't talk. My stepfather turns on the heat and then turns on the radio. John Lennon's singing *Imagine*.

When the song is over, Tatyana Alexeyevna starts talking:
"Sasha, last night you wanted to know what happened to my daughter."
"Yes, very much!"

Okay . . . why not . . . I think I stopped with me getting a good job. Reports, certificates, schedules. Every day I typed up documents, and from time to time my boss would walk around my desk dictating letters to his superiors:

DEAR SEMYON ZAKHAROVICH
THIS IS HOW THINGS ARE OVER HERE.
OUR MOST SERIOUS PROBLEM IS STILL THE LIVING QUAR-TERS. FEMALE PRISONERS LIVE IN BARRACKS THAT WERE NOT DESIGNED FOR LIVING. THEY ARE TERRIBLY CRAMPED. THERE IS LESS THAN ONE METER FOR EACH CONVICT. THE BUNKBEDS ARE STACKED SEVERAL LEVELS HIGH. IT WOULD BE FAIR TO SAY THERE IS MORE SPACE IN A COFFIN. AS YOU KNOW, THERE IS NO FLOOR OR ROOF. DUE TO POOR NUTRITION, THE PRISON-ERS FALL SICK AND DIE. OTHER THAN THAT, EVERYTHING IS GOING WELL HERE. WE ARE TRYING TO FULFILL THE PLAN.

I could have added a lot to that letter, but I typed quietly and tried to remember every word so that one day after my release I could tell people everything I'd heard. It's a pity that only after my release did I realize no one needed that truth . . .

Tatyana Alexeyevna falls silent for a moment. I look at my stepfather and notice he doesn't like this conversation. Uncle Grisha, however, pretends that he's fully occupied with driving.

Somehow or other, when I returned to the barracks, I would notice that some women weren't there anymore. Hunger, beatings, unbearable diseases. Here and there, to the other prisoners' delight, vacancies occasionally opened up on the bunks. There was a person, and now she's gone. "Remember, Tanya, we are nothing more than a species."

Tatyana Alexeyevna tried to come up with a solution that would help her find Asya. An island of the dead and destinies run aground. She would close her eyes and imagine that she was ironing sheets or bathing Asya or washing her clothes.

Now we all dreamed of doing the very chores that used to tire us out in those peaceful times. There, in the camp, we suddenly realized how dear and important it all was—everyday life. The regular rhythm of happiness, the recurring comfort of home. How I wanted to go back! But the long and frightening word 'rehabilitation' stood in my way. "There was nothing in your lives before now! There were no dinners or laughter, there were no friends! You are enemies of the people! Be happy you've been allowed to begin a new life!"

Ten months passed of this so-called rehabilitation. Then another twenty. Tatyana Alexeyevna still didn't know anything about her daughter's fate, and, year after year, as she typed the camp documents, she continued to celebrate Asya's birthdays, quietly and alone.

The octet became not only a new home for her, but a second university as well.

I graduated from Moscow State University but learned truly valuable things only there, in the camp. "Do you know what a dung beetle does in horse manure?" my bunkmate asked. "It builds a house for its offspring. A dung beetle is always in a hurry because manure dries very quickly in the sun. There's no time for deliberation—it needs to work before the opportunity passes. The female beetle makes a ball from manure and buries it in the ground, but before burying it, she molds it into a pear shape and puts an egg on top. A few days later, a larva appears and begins eating the pear from the inside. The larva will turn into a chrysalis, and the chrysalis will turn into a beetle. When the beetle emerges, it won't know what kind of house its parents had built for it, but it will build exactly the same kind of house for its offspring. In this way, comrades, we are not that different from beetles. We put others down not because we feel the necessity of doing so, but only because our fathers and grandfathers behaved in exactly that way. Genetic memory. We're born to injure and be injured."

"I still want to believe we're slightly different from dung beetles," I said, turning over.

One morning another neighbor, who, I learned later, was a prominent art historian, told me, "You know, Tanya, there is not a single indication in the Gospels of what Jesus Christ looked like. There's no description. We don't know how the son of God looked, but we have thousands of paintings and icons that have changed our perception of who he was. Now everybody thinks that we know what Jesus looked like. Long hair, short beard. If I ask you to draw him, you'd do so without any problem. The same is true with Stalin. No one knows how a real leader should look, but we were all brainwashed to think that a leader should look like Stalin. It's not that Stalin is a leader, but that every leader should be like Stalin. And this idea is more profound and powerful than we realize. I'm afraid that another fifty years will pass, even sixty, and people will still be under the delusion that Stalin was not a common thief who seized power but a leader. Unfortunately, primitive people don't see any difference between reality and a depiction of reality, and we're primitive."

"I saw him in person . . ."

"Stalin? Really? Where?!"

"He visited our department and talked in front of a small group of colleagues."

"And what does he look like in real life?"

"Not like his portraits. He spoke with a very strong Georgian accent, and he was always rocking back and forth. I looked at him thinking at any moment he'd fall backward."

"One day he will definitely fall!"

"It's hard to believe . . ."

Once, another bunkmate noticed Tatyana Alexeyevna drawing something on a small piece of paper and asked if she would draw her daughter.

It came out very well. Word spread through the octet, and I became the main portrait artist of the barracks. Getting hold of paper was as hard as getting food or alcohol, but the inmates' desire to have portraits of their children was so strong that the women were ready to exchange a week's supply of tobacco for the tiniest piece of paper. Almost every night, the inmates would sit next to me and describe their sons and daughters. Serious or high-spirited, chubby or thin. I drew hundreds of children's eyes. After I returned from work, I was no longer taking care of my own business but making sketches of the children kidnapped by the Soviet government.

I drew other women's children but never attempted to draw Asya. I don't know why. I was probably too afraid. And I was already afflicted with phantom pains. My daughter wasn't near, but I often heard her voice, felt her hands touching me. I remembered how she laughed, and from time to time, I fantasized that my daughter was running through the barracks. Honestly, I don't understand how I didn't go insane. Perhaps it was too early—I didn't yet know what was in store for me . . .

"There's an old truth," our barracks leader said as she gazed *at my drawing of her son. "A man lives as long as he has some business on this earth. If he has no responsibilities, he'll die right away. That means that all of us here, in the Gulag, are alive today only because somewhere, on the other side, our husbands and sons are waiting for us . . ."*

"Or not waiting," another woman said, the same woman who had told me a while ago about the dung beetle. "Maybe they're all are dead already. And if they're dead, then we don't have any business here. What are we supposed to do then?"

"Cry!"

"Cry? As if there weren't already enough tears on this earth without ours! For me, there's nothing left to do here!"

"What are you saying? What about your husband? And your children? Would you have landed here if your husband hadn't been arrested?"

"I don't have a husband anymore! I sense that he's gone! And my children are gone too! They're all in the ground, and I'll be there soon."

"How can you say such things?"

"Listen, maybe that's enough already, huh? Aren't you disgusted listening to all this? You go around making yourselves into saints and martyrs, like the wives of the Decembrists.[4] Don't you understand that none of our loved ones are still alive?"

Tatyana Alexeyevna listened to the women arguing but didn't join in the conversation. She understood that her husband had

[4] The Decembrists is a name given to a group of young Russian nobles who on December 26, 1825, led an armed uprising on Senate Square in St. Petersburg to force the line of succession to go to the late Tsar Alexander I's elder brother Constantine rather than to his brother Nicholas. Constantine, who had removed himself from the line of succession, was believed to be more liberal-leaning than Nicholas. Many of the Decembrists were exiled to Siberia and many of their wives followed them there. They were held up as models of self-sacrifice and devotion. [Translators' note]

most likely been executed, but her heart refused to believe it. She still hoped everything would turn out well.

I sensed that Alexey and Asya were alive and, therefore, I still had responsibilities on this earth. I believed that, in another few years, I'd be able to take my daughter from the orphanage and, together, we'd wait for her father, and I would sleep a maximum of one to two hours a day to make up for the time I'd spent in the camp. Asya would be sniffling at my side, and I'd sit close by and protect her sleep. I would think about my young daughter, forgetting that she was already fifteen years old.

In the spring of 1953, a week after Stalin's death, a magic word exploded over the camp: amnesty. Release was possible for pregnant women and for those whose children were in orphanages. There was even talk that for those convicted for more than five years, the term would be cut in half. After eight years in the Gulag, Tatyana Alexeyevna suddenly had a chance. The camp was in an unprecedented state of excitement, and Tatyana Alexeyevna rejoiced with the others. Those women who were not covered by the conditions of the amnesty begged the convoy guards to impregnate them, while Tatyana Alexeyevna worked in the office with particular zeal—for the first time in many years she wanted to thank the Soviet government. It was no small thing that, after so many years of separation, she was getting a chance to see her daughter again.

PRESIDIUM
OF THE SUPREME SOVIET OF THE USSR

27 MARCH 1953
AMNESTY DECREE

OBSERVANCE OF THE LAW AND OF THE SOCIALIST ORDER HAS GROWN STRONGER AND THE INCIDENCE OF CRIME HAS CONSIDERABLY DECREASED IN THE COUNTRY AS A RESULT OF THE CONSOLIDATION OF THE SOVIET CIVIL AND STATE SYSTEM, THE INCREASING WELLBEING AND CULTURAL LEVEL OF THE POPULATION, THE INCREASING CIVIC CONSCIOUSNESS OF SOVIET CITIZENS, AND OF THEIR HONEST ATTITUDE TOWARD THE PERFORMANCE OF THEIR CIVIC DUTIES.

THE PRESIDIUM OF THE SUPREME SOVIET OF THE USSR DEEMS THAT, IN THESE CIRCUMSTANCES, IT IS NO LONGER NECESSARY TO RETAIN IN PLACES OF DETENTION PERSONS WHO HAVE COMMITTED OFFENSES REPRESENTING NO GREAT DANGER TO THE STATE AND WHO HAVE SHOWN BY THEIR CONSCIENTIOUS ATTITUDE TOWARD WORK THAT THEY ARE FIT TO RETURN TO HONEST WORKING LIFE AND TO BECOME USEFUL MEMBERS OF SOCIETY.

THE PRESIDIUM OF THE SUPREME SOVIET OF THE USSR HEREBY DECREES:

1. PERSONS SENTENCED TO IMPRISONMENT FOR UP TO FIVE YEARS INCLUSIVE ARE TO BE RELEASED FROM PLACES OF DETENTION AND FREED FROM OTHER PUNITIVE MEASURES NOT CONNECTED WITH DEPRIVATION OF FREEDOM.

2. PERSONS SENTENCED, REGARDLESS OF THE DURATION OF THE SENTENCE, FOR OFFENSES COMMITTED IN AN OFFICIAL CAPACITY AND FOR ECONOMIC OFFENSES, AS WELL AS MILITARY OFFENSES STIPULATED IN ARTICLES 193-4A, 193-7, 193-8, 193-10, 193-10A, 193-14, 193-15, 193-16 AND 193-17A OF THE PENAL CODE OF THE RUSSIAN REPUBLIC AND CORRESPONDING ARTICLES OF ALL OTHER UNION REPUBLIC PENAL CODES ARE TO BE RELEASED FROM PLACES OF DETENTION.

3. WOMEN WHO HAVE CHILDREN OF UP TO TEN YEARS OF AGE; PREGNANT WOMEN; JUVENILE DELINQUENTS UP TO 18 YEARS OF AGE, MEN OVER 55 AND WOMEN OVER 50 YEARS OF AGE, AS WELL AS CONVICTED PERSONS SUFFERING FROM

GRAVE INCURABLE DISEASES, ARE TO BE RELEASED FROM PLACES OF DETENTION.

4. CONVICTS WHOSE SENTENCES INCLUDE DEPRIVATION OF FREEDOM FOR MORE THAN FIVE YEARS ARE TO HAVE THEIR SENTENCES REDUCED BY HALF.

5. ALL TRIALS IN PROGRESS AND ALL CASES YET TO BE HEARD BY COURTS ARE TO BE DISMISSED IF THEY INVOLVE THE FOLLOWING TYPES OF CRIMES COMMITTED BEFORE THE ISSUANCE OF THIS DECREE:

(A) CRIMES FOR WHICH THE LAW PRESCRIBES AS PUNISH-MENT THE DEPRIVATION OF FREEDOM FOR UP TO FIVE YEARS OR OTHER PENALTIES NOT CONNECTED WITH INCARCERATION IN PLACES OF DETENTION.

(B) CRIMES COMMITTED IN AN OFFICIAL CAPACITY, AND ECONOMIC AND MILITARY CRIMES LISTED IN ARTICLE 2 OF THIS DECREE.

(C) CRIMES COMMITTED BY PERSONS FITTING THE DESCRIPTIONS IN ARTICLE 3 OF THIS DECREE.

AS FOR OTHER CASES OF CRIMES COMMITTED BEFORE THE ISSUANCE OF THIS DECREE FOR WHICH THE LAW PRESCRIBES DEPRIVATION OF FREEDOM FOR MORE THAN FIVE YEARS, IF A COURT FINDS IT NECESSARY TO PASS A SENTENCE OF DEPRIVA-TION OF FREEDOM FOR NOT MORE THAN FIVE YEARS, IT SHALL RELEASE THE DEFENDANT FROM PUNISHMENT; AND, IF A COURT FINDS IT NECESSARY TO ISSUE A SENTENCE OF DEPRI-VATION OF FREEDOM FOR MORE THAN FIVE YEARS, IT SHALL REDUCE THE TERM BY HALF.

6. CITIZENS WHO HAVE BEEN TRIED IN THE PAST AND HAVE SERVED THEIR SENTENCES OR WHO HAVE BEEN RELEASED FROM PUNISHMENT ON THE BASIS OF THIS DECREE BEFORE COMPLE-TION OF THEIR SENTENCE SHALL HAVE THEIR CRIMINAL RECORD EXPUNGED AND THEIR VOTING RIGHTS RESTORED.

7. THIS AMNESTY SHALL NOT APPLY TO PERSONS SEN-TENCED TO TERMS OF MORE THAN FIVE YEARS FOR COUNTER-

REVOLUTIONARY CRIMES, MAJOR THEFT OF SOCIALIST PROP-
ERTY, BANDITRY, AND PREMEDITATED MURDER.

8. THE CRIMINAL LAWS OF THE USSR AND UNION REPUBLICS
ARE TO BE REEXAMINED WITH A VIEW TO SUBSTITUTING
ADMINISTRATIVE AND DISCIPLINARY MEASURES FOR CRIMINAL
RESPONSIBILITY IN CASES OF OFFENSES COMMITTED IN AN
OFFICIAL CAPACITY AND IN CASES OF ECONOMIC, PETTY
SOCIAL AND OTHER LESS DANGEROUS CRIMES, AND TO REDUC-
ING THE CRIMINAL RESPONSIBILITY FOR CERTAIN CRIMES.

THE MINISTRY OF JUSTICE OF THE USSR IS TO BE GIVEN
THE TASK OF DRAWING UP THE APPROPRIATE PROPOSALS
WITHIN A MONTH AND SUBMITTING THEM TO THE COUNCIL OF
MINISTERS OF THE USSR FOR REVIEW AND FOR PRESENTATION
TO THE PRESIDIUM OF THE SUPREME SOVIET OF THE USSR.

CHAIRMAN OF THE PRESIDIUM
OF THE SUPREME SOVIET OF THE USSR
K. VOROSHILOV
SECRETARY OF THE PRESIDIUM
OF THE SUPREME SOVIET OF THE USSR
N. PEGOV

But no, she didn't get that chance. The amnesty decree was
published on March 27. As Tatyana Alexeyevna read the first
six paragraphs, she couldn't breathe from happiness. But when
she read the seventh, she passed out.

When she came to, the radio was playing Tchaikovsky's
Fifth Symphony.

*I was lying on the floor for a long time, with my eyes shut;
only the camp warden was able to bring me to my senses.*

"Pavkova, why are you lying on the floor?"

"The seventh paragraph applies to me, right?"

*"Yes, my dear. All enemies of the people must complete their
rehabilitation."*

"That means criminals will be released, but I won't?"

"That means criminals will be released, and you won't—that's right."

"But how can that be?"

"Somehow it can, my dear, somehow it can. But don't think about going on strike! Here, have some water and get up. It's no good lying in the middle of my office. Or do you want to go to solitary confinement?"

One of God's jokes. Many years before, she had tried to save her family by crossing out her husband's name from the list of prisoners of war. In the spring of 1953, fate sent the boomerang back to her: she sat at her desk and typed the list of soon-to-be-released women, but her name wasn't on that list.

+

Her octet was empty by summer. Convict Pavkova lay on her bunk, looking at her surname scratched into the wood with a nail, and whispered to herself a poem by Georgy Ivanov:

It's good there is no Tsar.
It's good there is no Russia.
It's good there is no god.

Only the yellow dawn,
Only icy stars,
Only a million years.

It's good there's no one,
It's good there's nothing,
It's all so black and dead,

Blacker and more dead
It could never be,
No one's there to help us now
And to help us there's no need.

Another amnesty was announced a year later. This time they were releasing convicts who had served two thirds of their terms. Tatyana Alexeyevna was unlucky again—she'd served only nine out of her fifteen-year sentence. If, in 1953, she'd almost ended up in the prison hospital, this time she accepted her bad luck as something entirely logical.

Heraclitus said that life is death, but it seems to me now that Proust was right, not Heraclitus: Life is effort through time—it is a continuous attempt to survive.

As she sat in the office, she put down the documents she was working on and looked out the window, but there was nothing on the other side.

I was listening to Shostakovich, who for some reason on that day wasn't forbidden, and contemplating the fact that I would never be released. Staring at the German radio (after 1946 we received a lot of stuff, even dishes, from the Nazi concentration camps), I tried to imagine what my daughter looked like. The last time I saw her was in July of 1945. That was nine year ago. Nine years had passed. Asya was born in 1938. It was now 1954. My daughter had turned sixteen. How much does she weigh? What does she talk about? What are her hobbies? What are her likes and dislikes? Is she angry with the world or not? How tall is she? How does she talk? Does she look more like me or Lyosha? Does she still remember English? Lyosha! If only I could know where you are. Our daughter turns sixteen today.

Tatyana Alexeyevna was released in 1955. As if nothing had happened. They announced another amnesty but didn't remove her conviction from the records. "Farewell, Pavkova! Don't hold a grudge!"

They threw me out onto the other side but prohibited me from returning to Moscow. I could have just ignored them and gone anyway, but during all those years I hadn't even saved enough money for a ticket—my work in the office didn't count since I was working there unofficially. I didn't have any money, and I didn't have any place to stay. That was one of the most terrifying days of my life. I had spent ten years waiting to be released, but as soon I was free, I had to return to the camp of my own volition. After spending several hours outside the fence, I went to Podushkin and asked him to give me a job. The next morning, I was sitting at my desk again. But now I was free. Comrade Stalin's experiment had truly worked: For Soviet people, the real prison was not the elaborate penitentiary system— it was their own fate.

I was released, but I returned to the camp myself. "What are you complaining about, Pavkova? And you said it was bad here! We didn't invite you back, but you came anyway! You want to work here? Well, we don't know. We need to think about it . . . Okay, okay. We've been friends for so many years! Look how humane the Soviet Union is! Your rehabilitation was successful, and now we'll give you a salary and a room in a workers' dormitory. Celebrate, Pavkova, sing the praises of the leader and mourn his passing!"

I still couldn't go 'home,' but I finally got permission to write letters. I immediately took a day off, borrowed some money from my colleagues, and went to Sverdlovsk, to the Bureau of Addresses. Once there, I submitted three inquiries—one for my husband, one for my daughter, and one for Lyosha's parents.

"How long do I have to wait for an answer?"

"No one knows," a faceless woman calmly replied.

I realized that I shouldn't count on the address bureau alone. I sent letters to the MID, the MVD, and the KGB. I'd been writing to the courts, requesting that they expunge my criminal record and allow me to return to Moscow, and I'd been writing to all the orphanages I could find. I sent out an inquiry almost every day. If before I'd dreamed about the day of my release, now I waited impatiently for an official letter with the words 'your conviction is expunged.' I wanted to begin traveling, but I still didn't know where. Who would I find first: Lyosha or Asya? Where is he? Where is she? If Lyosha was sentenced to fifteen years, he still has five years left, if it was twenty-five—then there are ten years remaining. "But that's nothing, it's not important now. We survived the war—we'll survive this too!"

They expunged my conviction in 1957. The Soviet government didn't apologize, they just informed me. "You asked? We answered. Yes, there were isolated cases of overzealous prosecution. Perhaps it was too much punishment in your case. Do you want to live in Moscow? Okay, go back to Moscow."

I didn't return to Moscow. I went to Minsk. Except for my father's grave, there was nothing waiting for me in Moscow. In Minsk, I found Lyosha's mom. When I came here, I learned that she'd lost her husband—a drunken German officer killed him with a bottle to win a bet. My mother-in-law didn't know anything about her son's fate. I decided to live here, in this apartment. My mother-in-law offered to help me get a job as a translator at the Academy of Sciences, but I applied to the post office.

"What for?" asked Uncle Grisha, no longer hiding the fact that he'd been listening.

"I had a plan . . .

What skills did I have? I knew how to work with documents. What could the Soviet government threaten me with? Nothing. So, I began to dig into other people's letters. I wasn't interested in intrigues or family scandals. I was looking for people whose children had ended up in orphanages. I wanted to optimize my search. You need to keep in mind that no one was talking about this openly—Soviet citizens had learned the art of euphemism a long time ago, but there were some hints in the letters. Moreover, examining other people's correspondence allowed me to trace official inquiries. In the end, I was able to find a few dozen mothers who, just like me, were searching for their children.

After I put all the letters in the mailboxes and personally delivered the telegrams, I would go to those addresses that were of interest only to me. Without any prelude or overture, right at the door, I would announce what I'd come for. Yes, you're right, all this was happening in the proverbial Soviet era.

"I know that you were in the Gulag . . ."

"What?"

"I was there too. Was your daughter in an orphanage?"

"Yes."

"Can I come in?"

This was not a useless census but a true record of the population. The history of a country that was put through the Gulag. Tatyana Alexeyevna would go into the kitchen and explain that she still didn't know anything about her daughter.

I didn't even know if she was alive.

Some people invited her to sit down and told her everything they knew, while others would silently show her the door. Some people were no longer afraid, while others were sure they were being set up. A government of terrible secrets. The Union of Soviet Socialist Republics, which were, in reality, united only by terrible secrets. The horror of silence, a memorial society of the mute.

"Don't come here again!"

"Wait, I have something else to tell you . . ."

It was a chronic wound that everybody was trying to treat differently. Here is a plantain leaf, Tanya. Here's an antibiotic. And here's a slap in your face. Forget about it! Remember! Don't dig any deeper!

I remember I was once in a courtyard, and some new con-
struction caught my attention. At that moment, a young girl
started pulling on my mailbag:
"I know why you came here."
"Of course, you do! I deliver mail."
"Don't be silly. You came to find out how we've been living.
Do you think you're the first?"
"Aren't I?"
"Of course not. There've been others."
"Other mailmen?"
"Other moms . . ."

The Soviet state didn't think it was necessary to inform people about the fate of their relatives. "How would we know if
you need information or not? But if you need it, then what are
you waiting for—make an inquiry. But, honestly, what's the
point of stirring up the past? Who would benefit from that?
Why are you blubbering over all that as if you were the Red
Cross?"

Citizens who had gone through the Gulag tried to help her
in any way they could. Tatyana Alexeyevna took drawings of
her daughter with her everywhere.

Yes, I've made about a hundred of them now. Of course, I
could be wrong, but for some reason I believed Asya would look
like this.
"Here's Asya at ten, and here's Asya at fifteen."

If there was any opportunity, Tatyana Alexeyevna would
show her drawings to young people who might have been in
the same orphanage as her daughter.

"No, there was no one like that."

"I see. If possible, could you, please, tell me how things
were there?"

170 - SASHA FILIPENKO

"Under the first director we lived well, but when he got arrested too, things got worse."

I found out that the children were sent through the same prisoner transport system as we adults were, under a convoy of guards with German shepherds. The children would be given rations, and, of course, they had to work. Five times a week, five-year-old children were equipped with little hoes and sent to pull out weeds in the vegetable garden. Every work force, no matter how small, had to support the building of our great country.

I found out that the children would catch rats and eat them, and from their first days in the camp they learned to tell on each other, and to figure out which teachers were kind or mean, honest or crazy. Other people's children told me that some orphans publicly denounced their parents, and some would bury their faces in their pillows and quietly swear to spend the rest of their lives avenging their mothers and fathers.

That's how my travels through the Soviet Union began. I went to Perm and Kazakhstan, to Krasnoyarsk and Sverdlovsk, searching for my daughter. One after another, I visited all the orphanages where my daughter might have been, but still I couldn't find Asya.

"No, she wasn't here . . ."

Then I met Yadviga. Her husband was a Belorussian theater producer. He was executed in 1937, and her son was arrested in 1939. The Soviet state murdered those people only because they lived in Belorussia and dared to speak Belorussian, their native language. The national question. There is only one great nation here. Yadviga knew her husband's fate, but she couldn't find where her son was buried. We continued to search together.

I remember how we were sitting here, in this apartment, in April of 1961. A man had just returned from space. Yuri Gagarin stated that he didn't see any god there. When Yadviga heard that, she couldn't help taking a jab: "You don't need to fly into space

*for that—all he needed was a trip to the Gulag." By that time,
we already knew that her son had been shot dead attempting to
escape.*

*"We lost again," Yadviga said. "Now they'll hide behind this
victory and tell us that everything happened for a reason."*

"What happened for a reason?"

*"Everything. The execution of the Tsar's family, the White
Army officers who were put on ferries by the thousands and
drowned, Antonov's rebellion, burned villages, obliterated
poets, the Ukrainian famine, and the Gulag—now they'll keep
on saying forever that everything was done for a reason."*

"As if they couldn't have made it into space any other way."

"Unfortunately, the majority will always think like that."

Tatyana Alexeyevna stops talking. I look out the window. I
realize only now that we arrived a long time ago. I see my new
home, and Bulat Okydzhava is singing:

In those years of separation, in those years of defeat, when
no leniency could be expected from the pounding rains,
and the commanders had all grown hoarse . . . then people's
hopes were commanded by a little orchestra under the
direction of love.

A little orchestra under the direction of love.

"Anyway, what happened to your daughter?" Uncle Grisha
asks, interrupting Okudzhava.

"What happened to my daughter?"

"Yeah," my stepfather says and turns toward Tatyana
Alexeyevna who's sitting behind him in the backseat.

"You're probably expecting an interesting story from me,
right? Something captivating and intriguing?"

"We're expecting the truth."

"The truth? But who needs that?"

"The majority of the people here in this gas-guzzling machine?"

"It sounds funny . . . in this machine. In this damned machine that ground me to bits. My daughter . . . My daughter . . ."

The truth was that her daughter had died . . . from hunger. She never made it to sixteen, or even ten. She died from malnutrition in the winter of 1946. During all those years Tatyana Alexeyevna spent in the camp, her daughter was lying in the cold ground, in a common grave, along with other children. The Soviet state provided neither a coffin nor a cross for her. Only a small plaque with a number on it. In the official statement the cause of death was listed as a heart defect. In the 1970s, Tatyana Alexeyevna found the orphanage in Kazakhstan where Asya had been sent. Tatyana Alexeyevna saw the accommodations where her daughter slept along with sixty other children of enemies of the people; she saw the vegetable patch they used to weed. They showed this mother a picture of her daughter looking at this world with frightened eyes, and they took her to her place of burial.

I asked if I could put a cross there, but they told me that crosses weren't allowed.

I thought, to hell with them, and found some guy in a garage and asked him to make a cross. This Kazakh welded a cross out of two rusty pipes and, despite the director's ban, helped me plant it in the ground. Every year, I fly to Kazakhstan and check on the cross. The cross is still there. Narrow and of human height. Simple but proud. Exactly what I wanted.

"And your husband?" Uncle Grisha asks, interrupting Tatyana Alexeyevna again.

"He was executed when I was in prison. Later I learned that after Lyosha was captured, he worked as a draftsman for the Germans. He copied seized Soviet documents, and that saved him from death in the camp. But it didn't save him from the Soviet state."

"So it's all true! He was released, and they executed him because he'd worked for the enemy!"

"Uncle Grisha . . ."

"It's okay, Sasha, let him talk."

"What don't you understand, Uncle Grisha? She told us herself that her husband worked for the fascists."

"Yes, just imagine. He was taken prisoner, and, in the camp, he agreed to copy Soviet documents to save his life. I'm sure you would have behaved totally differently in his place. If you don't mind, I'd like to go now. How do I open your door?"

After Tatyana Alexeyevna leaves, my stepfather continues:

"She's lying about everything. Most likely no one harmed her daughter. She should thank the state for taking care of her daughter while she was in prison. They could've left the girl on the street. The old lady has probably gone nuts. There weren't any purges—it's all baloney. I saw a documentary. Stalin tried to save the country, and now these rotten democracy-lovers intentionally falsify documents and put them into the archives in order to smear the party. But it won't work here, not in our Belorussia. Our leader won't allow it!"

I thank my stepfather for his help and climb the stairs. At home, without even taking my shoes off, I go straight to the kitchen and open the fridge. I grab the bottle of vodka, remove the cap, and take a swig.

Now I know my neighbor's story. I remember how she arrived in the Soviet Union and entered the university, how she fell in love and became a mom. I know that Tatyana Alexeyevna lost everything, but there's one thing I still don't understand: After learning her husband's and daughter's fate back in the 1970s, why didn't she commit suicide? If a period had been placed at the end of her life thirty years ago, then why, after so many tragedies, does she go on living? What for?

I turn off the light, close the door, but don't make it to my neighbor's door—Lera's in the way. She's standing there with a laptop in her hands.

"I brought the comedy!"

"Right . . ." I answer, stepping back.

To be honest, I'm happy she's stopped by. I find Lera's concern touching. It's been months since anyone's been interested in me. Lera goes into the living room, puts the computer on the table, and turns on the movie. We sit on the new coach. Furniture without a history. Before ten minutes have passed, my young neighbor suddenly hits the pause key and kisses me. We're not divine creatures, just a species of animal. I think to myself, God bless Belorussia!

After everything is over, we lie on the floor and look at the ceiling. Lera puts her head on my arm, kisses my shoulder, and asks:

"What are you thinking about?"

"About going to Mars."

"How long does it take to get there?"

"Nine months."

"Nine months . . . Oho . . . that's enough time to have a baby."

"Sometimes it takes less time . . ."

"To have a baby?"

"To get to Mars."

"And what's there to do on Mars?"

"Build a new life."

"Why don't you do it here?"

"It's not possible anymore."

"Why's that?"

"The past won't allow it."

"But whoever flies to Mars can't go there without a past. It's impossible to colonize a new planet without making use of previously acquired knowledge."

"And that's our main problem. We have to decide what to do with a man who's completely exhausted himself."

"Exhausted? Don't be silly! We're just getting to know each other."

"We're getting to know each other, but man was finished a long time ago. Nothing new can happen with us anymore. The expedition to Mars will fail if we send an old man there."

"It's impossible to start a new life if you've forgotten your old one."

"It's impossible, but that's the only way."

+

A few weeks later, I'm lying in bed. My daughter is still sleeping, which is why I can allow myself to drink some coffee and watch a little TV. Channel One is showing *The Word of the Preacher*. The Metropolitan is talking about the cross:

"In the symbolism of the Gospels, the cross represents suffering and pain born by circumstances that are impossible to overcome.

"There are many examples of self-sacrifice for the sake of a higher purpose, a high ideal, and the greater good. A soldier bears the hardship of war with courage and patience. He sacrifices his life to serve his country and the cause of victory, and often commits deeds of heroism—the highest degree of self-sacrifice. A mother sacrifices her own wellbeing for the good of her children, experiences overwhelming hardships, difficulties, and sorrows, which often exceed her natural strength.

"And so, a person's ability to carry their cross is nothing more than an expression of their internal strength.

"However, in many cases, people are responsible for their own sorrow and misfortune. A person makes mistakes, sets false goals, becomes a victim of their own frivolity, inexperience, or bad intentions. They engage in conflict with their close friends and family, suffers from their own indiscretion, and so on. Such hardships are not a person's cross, because all those misfortunes could have been avoided.

"The Gospels and the history of the Church are a testament

to the fact that a cross, if it is a true cross of God, will never be too heavy to bear."

"Well, how about that!" I think. At this moment my daughter wakes up, and I turn off the TV.

+

Her illness progresses. Tatyana Alexeyevna is departing. We meet every day, and every conversation reveals new problems. The eraser of memory. The scissors of fate. My neighbor no longer remembers that she was born in London and moved to Soviet Russia. She's forgotten her father's name and the name of the school she went to in Moscow. I realize that I have only a few weeks left and so will try to spend all my free time with Tatyana Alexeyevna.

"Is this your wife?"

"No, this is Lera, she lives one floor down. Do you remember her?"

"No."

"Do you mind if she has tea with us?"

"Of course not! I'd be very glad."

"You told me yesterday that in the middle of the 1970s you tried to adopt a child."

"Yes. A boy and a girl. I wanted to help kids who were destined to spend their childhood in a Soviet orphanage."

"Did you succeed?"

No. My application was refused. They had several reasons for that. First, it was the opinion of the review committee that I was too old. Second, my past raised some doubts.

"*Please, forgive my asking, Comrade Pavkova, but I'd like to know: Where is your husband?*"

"*You know he was executed.*"

"So, you're a widow . . . Can we really place children into a home without a father?"

"I feel I have a lot of love in me."

"What you feel is of no concern to us. We are going to entrust you with the future of our Soviet children."

"I'm sure I can be a good mother to them."

"We must be sure that you'll succeed. How long did you spend in the Gulag?"

"Ten years."

"Ten years! But this does leave a mark, comrades! It's hard even to imagine what that could lead to . . ."

"What are you suggesting?"

"Why are you so irritated, Comrade Pavkova?"

"I'm not irritated, I just want you to stop playing this stupid game! What else do you need from me? You think I haven't been humiliated enough? You took away my daughter and my husband, you took away ten years of my life and stole my future, and now you want something more? Then just say so! I'll give it to you! The Soviet Union has taught me to give away everything. What do you want me to say now? Why are you doing this to me?"

"No one is doing anything to you, Comrade Pavkova. You've just demonstrated to the committee that you have a short temper. Personally, I'm not sure that such a person is capable of being a good mother."

I got up and left. I couldn't take it any longer. I'm not trying to say it was the right thing to do. I realize that, for the sake of those kids in the orphanage, I should have sucked it up and passed the test, but I couldn't.

"Have you ever had thoughts of suicide?"

"What?!"

"I'm asking, with everything you had to go through, why didn't you commit suicide?"

"Because after my breakdown in the prison hospital I

promised myself that I would live out the time that was granted to me. I had to find my husband and daughter. Once I'd learned about their deaths, I had to find their graves. The simple fact that my husband had become a prisoner of war gave me things to do for the rest of my life. I wanted to help other mothers and, of course, to find him one day . . ."

"To find who?"

"The man I set up. You ask why I haven't committed suicide, and I can give you an easy answer: I continued living only because there was one final piece of business for me on Earth—I had to find that unknown soldier and ask for his forgiveness."

"But what did you want to apologize for?" Lera asked suddenly.

"Are you familiar with my story?"

"Yes, Sasha told me about it."

"Then why are you asking?"

"I'm asking because I don't understand what you would apologize for. What did you do that is so wrong you need to apologize for it?"

"I filled in the last name of another man."

"And so what? Could it have really changed anything? Are you seriously worried about it a half century later?"

"Wouldn't you worry about it?"

"No, of course not! What a silly idea! What's so wrong with what you did? I'd understand if you came up with a random name and it'd turned out to be a real person, and he was arrested because of you. I'd understand if you personally convicted someone to death. But you, as far as I understand, haven't done that. So what if you filled in the name of some soldier twice? What difference could it have made? He was already on the list. Do you understand that you haven't really affected anything? Do you think he could've been prosecuted twice? Sent to the Gulag twice? Do you think the Chekists

would have searched for him with such zeal in order to exe-
cute him twice? I truly don't understand—have you really
been upset for so many years over such a little thing?"

"I thought I put a magnifying glass over his name."

"But that's nonsense! That's not what happened!"

"Even more so, I worried that I'd become an accomplice in
crime. There was a list made by fate, and there was a name that
I personally added to that list."

"Well, and so what? You added it, and so be it! There was
a list, you put one name on it twice, but your action could not
have influenced anyone or changed anything. So where is the
crime in all that?"

"For fifty years I considered it to be a crime of conscience."

"But that's not what happened, not at all! You didn't add
that last name, you simply entered it twice. It's like shooting a
corpse. But shooting a corpse is vandalism, not murder."

"It's only vandalism if at the moment you shoot, you know
the man is already a corpse, but when I was altering that list, I
didn't know that . . ."

I take Lera's hand, and she realizes that it's better to stop
talking. Tatyana Alexeyevna looks out the window for several
seconds, and, after a heavy pause, she continues her story:

*Well, one way or another, even though I was a total fool in
your opinion, I began my final search. After I found the burial
sites of Lyosha, Asya, and even Pasha Azarov, I realized that I
had only one battle left. I had to find out about the fate of the
man whose name I'd typed twice.*

"And you began sending new requests?"

*Yes. I was compiling new petitions, but this case was more
complicated because I remembered only his last name and his
initials. However, I think we'd better end this conversation . . .*

"No, Tatyana Alexeyevna, please! Lera didn't mean anything."

"There's no need to speak for me. I meant exactly what I said, but I didn't want to upset you. I truly don't understand what you're blaming yourself for."

"Tatyana Alexeyevna, please, tell us how you managed all those years."

How did I live? Normally. As long as my hands remembered the typewriter keys, I helped produce samizdat. Yadviga and I helped other relatives find their loved ones, and believe me, Sasha, sometimes getting information from our archives was harder than rescuing a person from the Gulag. I spent almost all my free time drawing, and by the end of the 1980s, I'd done so many paintings that Yadviga suggested I put on an exhibition. I took that idea as a joke, but my friend insisted. And so, after the fall of the Soviet Union, my canvases started traveling. I think in 1993 I was with my paintings in Milan. I remembered that only a hundred kilometers away, on Lake Lugano, my dear Romeo was waiting for me, and so I went to the small city of Porlezza. You'll laugh, but I found him. After sixty plus years, we were again sitting in the same San Michele park. The hotel where I once hid from him didn't exist anymore, but the lake and the mountains were still there. What beauty! Now it was simply impossible to believe that old story. Romeo couldn't remember who I was right away, but then he told me that he'd waited for me in the nearby cafe for several weeks.

"And after that?"

And after that, everything, of course, was forgotten. "Were you happy?" *I asked him in Italian.*

"Happy? Yes, I guess I was, overall. I have a good family, three children and eight grandchildren. I opened my own shop. I fix cars with my oldest son. My middle son moved to Florence, *and the youngest lives in Locarno. Yes, I think I'm happy. My life has been going pretty well, the only thing is—we weren't happy with our team. As you know, our village wasn't big enough to have a decent soccer club, so I supported Bologna. Before the war, they were champions five times, but after the war, they made me happy only once. If I could change anything in my life, I would've probably picked another team. But what about you? Do you have family?"*

"Yes, I had one . . ."

"Did you come to Porlezza just to see me?"

"I don't even know why I came. I simply happened to be nearby. Do you remember why we broke up?"

"No. I think something upset you. Do you remember?"

"Uh-uh," I lied.

I traveled a lot. I don't know what for, but I managed to visit almost all of Europe. Portraits of Asya and Lyosha are now in private collections in Berlin and Stuttgart, Copenhagen and Lyon. It seems that only here, in Minsk, no one needs them. Several years ago, I had an exhibition in Geneva. On a free day, I went to the archives of the Red Cross. There was no need to make arrangements in advance or to wait for many months to get permission. I just said that I wanted to see their correspondence with the Soviet Union, they took me to a small office, and the clerk put several boxes in front of me. I began to go through the letters I'd been sending them, and among other documents I found the list where the Swiss described in minute detail the fate of letters and telegrams sent to the USSR.

Telegram
23 June 1941   To the People's Commissar of Foreign Affairs offering our help to the USSR and making the ICRC's assets available for their use; asks the USSR to compile lists of

the wounded and the prisoners of war so we can pass these lists to the other side.

Telegram
24 June 1941

To the Executive Committee of the Soviet Red Cross and Red Crescent Societies informing them that yesterday a telegram was sent to Molotov with an offer of help under any circumstances. (Not answered)

Telegram
9 July 1942

To the People's Commissar informing him that Marcel Junod left for Ankara and that Germany, Finland, Hungary, and Romania agreed to exchange the POW lists according to our telegram of 27 June.

Telegram
22 July 1941

To the People's Commissar informing him that Italy and Slovakia agreed to exchange the lists of POWs and wounded soldiers on the basis of reciprocity, and that Italy is ready to acknowledge the convention on POWs. Requests an answer regarding the present issue and informs him of Dr. Junod's arrival in Ankara. (The answer arrived on August 8 from Vyshinsky.) (A similar telegram was sent to the Executive Committee of the Soviet Red Cross and the Red Crescent Societies.)

Telegram
8 August 1941

From Vyshinsky, the First Deputy of the People's Commissariat of Foreign Affairs, informing us that the USSR acknowledges the necessity of honoring the Hague Convention and agrees to an exchange of information concerning the POWs; however, indirectly, he refuses to apply the POW convention (see attachment).

Letter
15 August 1941

To the People's Commissar conveying to him a special note regarding the principles for the exchange of information concerning the POWs that were accepted by all sides. (Not answered)

(A similar telegram was sent to the Executive Committee of the Soviet Red Cross and the Red Crescent Societies on August 22, 1941. Not answered.)

Telegram
22 August 1941

To the People's Commissar informing him that Finland is ready, upon mutual agreement, to accept the Hague Convention and that Finland has formed its own Division of the Red Cross. (Not answered)

Telegram
22 August 1941

From the CIA in Moscow to Dr. Junod in Ankara passing on clarifications regarding the completed lists and announcing that the POWs captured by the USSR are allowed to send their families information regarding their captivity.

Telegram
28 August 1941   To the People's Commissar informing him that Romania has acknowledged the Hague Convention and compiled lists of Soviet POWs. (Not answered)

Telegram
18 September 1941   To the People's Commissar requesting an agreement from the representative in Iran to aid in the evacuation of the German civilian population.

Telegram
25 September 1941   To the People's Commissar requesting visas for Junod and Ramseier. (Not answered)

Telegram
25 September 1941   To the Executive Committee of the Soviet Red Cross and the Red Crescent Societies requesting that the lists be sent as soon as possible and that we receive a response to our earlier request for visas for our representatives. (Not answered)

Telegram
1 October 1941   To the Executive Committee of the Soviet Red Cross and the Red Crescent Societies offering mediation from the Rescue Service for sending collective parcels, food and clothes to Russian POWs; contains information regarding the possibility of making purchases for the Soviet side; requests that Article 15 of the Hague

Convention be applied on the basis of reciprocity to the German POWs in the
USSR with the purpose of sending them
said parcels. (Not answered)

Letter
13 November 1941 To Vinogradov at the Embassy in Ankara
providing 279 lists from the Romanian
side, prepared by the government of this
country without mutual agreement. (Not
answered)

Letter
14 November 1941 To Prince Karl informing him of the agreement with the USSR to exchange POWs
and of the fact that Russia did not send us
any lists and did not respond to our offer
of sending our representative.[5] Asks
Prince Karl for his suggestions and recom-
mendations. (Not answered)

Telegram
14 November 1941 To the Executive Committee of the Soviet
Red Cross and the Red Crescent Societies
and the Embassy of the USSR in Ankara
requesting a valid address for the Executive
Committee of the Soviet Red Cross and the
Red Crescent Societies; informs them that
the Italian authorities are treating the

[5] Prince Karl (as spelled in the original French document) most likely
refers to Prince Carl Eduard, Duke of Saxe-Coburg and Gotha and grandson
of Queen Victoria of England. He served as head of the German Red Cross
under Hitler. [Translator's note]

Russian POWs in the same way they treat POWs of other nationalities; reminds them that our delegation in Ankara sent them the POW lists from Germany, Romania, and Italy. (Not answered)

Telegram
20 November 1942 To the People's Commissar and the Executive Committee of the Soviet Red Cross and the Red Crescent Societies informing them that we received the lists containing 2,894 names of Soviet POWs in Romania and that the government of Romania will postpone future shipments of parcels until a mutual agreement is reached. (Not answered)

Letter
21 November 1941 From Miss Quinche to Miss Kollontai, the Soviet Ambassador in Stockholm, reminding her of the ICRC request to the Russian authorities and the importance of providing a visa for Dr. Junod. (Not answered)

Letter
2 December 1941 From Mr. Burckhardt to Mr. Maisky reminding him of yesterday's conversation regarding the ICRC actions and the question of visas for our delegates.

Telegram
6 December 1941 To the Executive Committee of the Soviet Red Cross and the Red Crescent Societies and the Embassy of the USSR in Ankara confirming the receipt in Geneva of the

list of 400 injured and sick Russian citizens in Finland, which we have a right to convey only in the event of a counterproposal from the USSR. (Not answered)

18 December 1941   Conversation between the diplomatic representative of the USSR in London and Mr. Burckhardt regarding the list of candidates for the position of our representative in the USSR, which will be favorably studied by the Soviet authorities.

Letter
7 January 1942   From the Red Cross of the USA (Norman Davis) containing information regarding the readiness of the German side and expressing concern over the inactivity of the Russians.

Telegram
14 January 1942   To the People's Commissar, Mr. Maisky and Miss Kollontai containing a list of the Swedish and Swiss representatives who are ready to leave for the USSR as a result of the negotiations with Maisky. (Not answered)

Telegram
5 February 1942   To the People's Commissar containing a proposal to provide the Russian POWs in Germany and Romania with sugar and a request regarding the possibility of shipping parcels to the German POWs in the USSR. (Not answered)

Telegram
27 February 1942   To the People's Commissar containing a
                    proposal to provide vitamins to the
                    Russian POWs and information regarding
                    the agreement of the Germans to distrib-
                    ute vitamins under the supervision of our
                    representatives under the condition that
                    the ICRC delegation be allowed to enter
                    Russia. (Not answered)

Letter
9 March 1942   To Mr. Winant, alerting him to the fact
                    that we have not received any answer from
                    the USSR regarding the approval of the
                    candidates; the Soviet authorities did not
                    even state their opinion regarding the
                    principles of this mission.

Telegram
1 April 1942   To the People's Commissar containing a
                    proposal from the Romanian government
                    to repatriate the badly wounded on a
                    reciprocal basis. (Not answered)

Telegram
23 July 1942   To Mr. Molotov requesting information
                    regarding the demand of the Finnish gov-
                    ernment concerning POWs; offers to
                    exchange the lists; points out that the pro-
                    posal to send a delegation was not
                    answered; offers basic exchange of infor-
                    mation. (The letter was sent through
                    Courvoisier and went unanswered.)

Letter
24 July 1942   To Mr. Molotov conveying the request of the Finnish government regarding the exchange of information (Article 14 of the Hague Convention and Article 4 of the Geneva Convention); proposes an exchange of information through our delegation in Ankara in the form of a synchronized exchange; and the provision on a reciprocal basis of information regarding captives to fighting parties. Memorandum attached. (Not answered)

Letter
28 August 1942   To Mr. Molotov regarding the proposal made by Romanian authorities to exchange 1,018 incapacitated Russian POWs for information regarding Romanian POWs. (Not answered)

Telegram
5 October 1942   To the Executive Committee of the Soviet Red Cross and the Red Crescent Societies conveying information regarding a visit to the Russian POW camps in Finland in July and August of the current year and distribution on site of parcels from America. Inform the competent Soviet agencies.

I put the list aside, wiped away my tears, and asked the archivist a question. More than fifty years later, I asked the question that my colleague had once addressed to me in the corridors of the NKID:

"Why were you doing this?"

"In what sense?"

"Why were you writing us all those letters?"

"What do you mean?"

"Why were you sending us all those letters when you saw that we didn't want to bring home a thousand of our own POWs even in exchange for unimportant information?!"

"Because this is what our humanitarian mission is all about. Moreover, I can assure you, my colleagues could not believe that you really didn't give a damn about your own soldiers. Many Red Cross officers naively thought that Moscow wasn't answering only because we hadn't properly filled out the documents."

"And in spite of all that, you continued writing . . ."

"We have always believed that there might be one person in any government or organization who would respond. Nine people might not answer, but the tenth might read it and try to do something."

"Unfortunately, you underestimated us."

You asked why I kept on living. How over the course of those thirty years I found the energy to go on. On that day in Geneva, I asked myself the same question. Why am I still alive? I lived because I was waiting. For thirty years, I'd been waiting for the official letter that would let me be at peace with myself. The only thing I wanted now was to know the fate of that unknown soldier. And on December 31, 1999, just a few hours before the New Year, a mailman rang my doorbell.

+

I couldn't believe my eyes. A man handed me a letter, and then he was gone. But how could he understand the miracle he'd brought me? I went to the kitchen and sat down. For a long time, I couldn't bring myself to open the envelope. Finally, I did and learned that the man whom I'd been seeking for more than thirty years was alive! I think the only other time I was so happy was the day I saw Lyosha's name on that list. I called Yadviga, and she came over. We quickly got ready and left for the airport. Minsk–Moscow, Moscow–Perm. We celebrated the new year at the airport.

One dark morning, we entered that small town. I broke down in tears. I had lived in a town like this after I was released from prison. A town that's built around a prison is a scary place. That soil is dead.

The taxi driver brought us to the right house at seven thirty in the morning. A dog was barking in the backyard. I thought it would be rude to visit so early, but a light was suddenly turned on inside the house. Yadviga was afraid of the dog, but the mutt was on a chain, and, after so many years in the Gulag, I could easily estimate a dog's threat. The dog was ugly but not scary, not dangerous, even for a ninety-year-old lady. I walked down the beaten path to the front door and knocked. A few moments later, an old man opened the door.

"Vyacheslav Viktorovich Pavkin?"

"Yes."

"May we come in?"

He didn't answer. I instantly understood that the man standing in front of me was that soldier. People who've been in captivity don't ask unnecessary questions. I asked to enter, and he let me in.

Vyacheslav Viktorovich sat on a chair and put his hands on his lap. We were still in the mud room. I stepped forward, and Yadviga came in behind me. It was hot, but I didn't dare take off my coat. He looked at us silently.

"Were you in captivity in Romania?"

"Yes," Pavkin answered, not with his voice but just by nodding.

"I worked at the NKID during the war. We once received a list of prisoners of war, and your name was on it. Unfortunately, my husband's name was on that list too. His name was listed right after yours. On that day, I got very scared and decided that if I didn't delete my husband's name, I'd be arrested for sure. The wife of an enemy of the people—of course, you remember those words. I had access to secret documents, and I was afraid for my daughter . . ."

Vyacheslav Viktorovich looked at me in silence. He was nodding his head very slightly, but I couldn't understand if it was a tic or a sign of agreement. In any case, he was listening to me attentively, so I continued talking.

"After I read the document, I decided to delete my husband from the list. I realized that the list would go to the NKVD, so I decided to leave my husband's name out and list your name twice. I didn't know you, didn't know if you had any children or family, but with that I was putting you and your family under a double threat. I tried to save myself and my own husband, but I put you in danger."

Pavkin still wasn't saying anything. I was looking at him and trying to be tactful. Believe me, Alexander, even at ninety, a person who's suffered so much is capable of feeling worried. I was looking at a man the same age as myself and trying to find the right words.

"I've been looking for you for thirty years. In the 1970s, I began writing inquiries to every place I could think of, searching for people from the Romanian list. But just yesterday, I received the letter stating that you were alive. Your address was in that letter, and I flew here without hesitating."

"What for?"

I realized why he'd asked that question. The most difficult moment was approaching. After so many years, I had to repent, to ask forgiveness for what I'd done. But was there any sense in all this? It was the year 2000. He was over eighty years old. Can I bring his family back to him?

"So why did you come here?" he turned toward me and asked again.

"To apologize . . ."

"But for what?"

I understood that, by asking this question, Pavkin probably wanted me to spell out everything and to leave no gaps.

"I came to apologize for what I'd done. At the beginning of the war, when I received the list of POWs, I transcribed it incorrectly. I deleted my husband's name and typed your name twice. I came to apologize for altering that list."

"But what list?"

"The list that put your family under threat of arrest . . ."

"But my family wasn't arrested."

"What do you mean?"

"Just what I said. My family wasn't arrested!"

"But you were in a Romanian POW camp?"

"I was. First, I was in a Romanian camp, then in other camps."

"Did you know that the list went to the NKVD, and that they were arresting all the relatives of the POWs?"

"No, I didn't know anything about that. I was freed in 1945, and I returned home. No one persecuted my family, and no one was arrested. My wife died five years ago from a heart attack, and my son and grandchildren live in Arkhangelsk."

"So, you and your relatives weren't purged?"
"I'm telling you, no!"

I broke down in tears. From happiness for this man and for the vagaries of my own fate. You're right, Lera, I was a complete fool. Sometimes it takes half a century to realize you were mistaken. I went down a wrong path. Thousands of kilometers toward a dead end. Since 1941, I'd been blaming myself for putting another person in danger, and only a year ago in Pavkin's house, I learned that the Romanian list didn't result in any arrests.

We left his house and went to the main square. The taxi driver was waiting for us near the Stalin monument. During our short conversation, someone had chopped off the leader's small head. I asked the taxi driver to take us back to the airport, and the car started off along the snowy road.

I think I told you that many years ago, back in the camp, I created a god for myself. I think I also told you that I got Alzheimer's only because that god was afraid to meet me. When I came back from the Perm region, that sweet woman, the realtor that sells apartments in our building, told me that I was losing my memory only because God loves me. In her opinion, God is merciful, and that's how he's showing his kindness at the end of my life. As if he was helping me by erasing the most painful memories, as if he was rewarding me . . .

Well, that's the opinion of a woman who sells apartments. She thinks this illusionist can cheat me, but it's not so. I assure you, Sasha, that when I get up there, I'm a thousand percent sure that no matter how hard he tries, I won't forget anything, ever.

+

Tatyana Alexeyevna dies on December 7. The realtor, my mother, Lera, and I attend the funeral. There are also a few artists there and some of the owners of her paintings. Her friend Yadviga doesn't come to the funeral. She's been sick for the last several months. I don't know if she welcomes her illness or not, but I visit her from time to time.

Tatyana Alexeyevna is no longer among us. Her apartment is waiting for a new owner, and every time I see the red cross on her door, I can't help asking: Why was Pavkin allowed to go home while Tatyana Alexeyevna's husband was executed?

My neighbor told me that those soldiers spent all those years together—together they were sent from one camp to another, and together they were released in 1945. They should have also returned home together, but one soldier for some reason was killed and the other was set free and decorated by the Soviets.

This question gave me no rest. So, when I went to Yekaterinburg to visit my wife's grave, I asked my friend to lend me his car for the day. I drove to that little town and saw the statue of Stalin with a new, disproportionally big head. I found Pavkin's house and knocked. A few moments later, a skinny old man opened the door.

"Vyacheslav Viktorovich?" I ask.

"Yes."

"Hello! I came from Yekaterinburg to see you. Can we talk?"

"Well, sure."

I enter. The house is decrepit. It's a lonely man's shack. The first thing I notice is a portrait of Stalin on the wall.

"You know, I'd like to ask you one question . . ."

"Well, go on."

"Do you remember a soldier, Alexey Pavkov, who was in captivity with you?"

"Well, let's say I remember him, so what?"

"What can you tell me about him?"

"What do you want to know?"

"Everything. What kind of soldier was he?"

"First of all, Pavkov was never a soldier. I was a soldier, but he only planned sabotage operations."

"I'm sorry, I didn't put it correctly. So, you remember him?"

"And if I do, so what?"

"Do you know how his life ended?"

"How is it any business of mine how his life ended? We weren't friends."

"And still . . . Do you know that he was executed by a firing squad?"

"And so what?"

"Do you really not give a damn about a man who spent so many years with you in captivity?"

"Listen, we lived in the same barracks, but every day I did the heavy lifting while he sat in a warm office among the Krauts drawing. I worked myself to death, and that self-serving bastard would come back to the barracks and say that it all happened because of Comrade Stalin, that Comrade Stalin is as much of a monster as Hitler. In the next camp, I was again killing myself with hard work, and that sponger found another cushy job for himself! He was a louse, that's what he was! That Pavkov was a dirty traitor and a rat!"

"I see. And after you were liberated from captivity, were you in a Soviet filtration camp?"

"Of course, I was! Like everyone else! But I hadn't committed any sins against the Soviet state, so they let me go right away."

"What do you mean they let you go?"

"Just that! Right away they made me an offer to collaborate, and I told them everything just like it happened. About your Pavkov, and about other anti-Soviets like him. Now they say there were purges, that they were all sent to the Gulag and executed, but nothing like that happened! They called me for an interrogation only twice, they were very polite to me, and after I told them everything, they sent me home. The Soviet state never prosecuted honest people!"

"And how many people went home with you?"

"I don't know, I was released alone."

The old man goes outside. I go after him. He takes a shovel, and I get into the car. The old man marches along the snowy road for a long time. I ask if he needs a ride, but he refuses. Finally, we find ourselves on the main square. I understand that the old man has come here to shovel the snow from around the leader's monument.

+

A year after Tatyana Alexeyevna's death, I go to a gravestone mason. I give him a small piece of paper and ask if he's able to engrave such an epitaph.

"Have you already picked out a headstone?"

"Yes, I would like it to be a cross made of red granite."

"Okay, no problem. And we'll do the engraving, that's not a problem."

A few days later, the cross is ready. I order the delivery and installation. The craftsmen work skillfully and quickly.

It's a warm, dry November day. We're at the Severnoe cemetery. The leaves are rustling in the trees above the gravestone. Rays of sun fall on the engraving carved in the cross, and I read her last words, directed to us all:

DON'T TREAD ON MY SOUL

+